MURDER IN
MALDIVES

Introducing
Detective Devin Langhar

SANCHITA SARIN

INDIA • SINGAPORE • MALAYSIA

Notion Press

Old No. 38, New No. 6
McNichols Road, Chetpet
Chennai - 600 031

First Published by Notion Press 2019
Copyright © Sanchita Sarin 2019
All Rights Reserved.

ISBN 978-1-64733-893-0

To Harsh, for having my back.

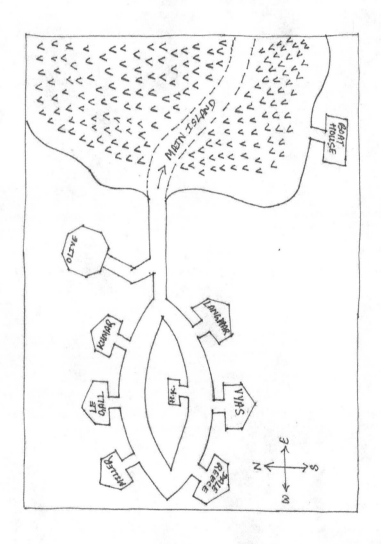

1

The Sun was hidden behind tall palm trees, having started its journey for today a few hours ago. The yellow glow escaping from between the trunks and the green leaves on the east side, established the presence of the invisible orb. The sky was akin to a smooth river, with no clouds hindering the soft blue and it stretched for as far as the eye could see; nothing man-made or nature-made stopping its course.

Soft morning light illuminated the turquoise water to its full glory. Lodged in a gigantic lagoon, surrounding the island on all sides- the colour was vibrant and yet transparent like a crystal; the shallow ocean bed visible for naked appreciation.

The brilliance of the Sun was the norm at this secluded island. Not another speck of land was visible for kilometres, and yet one didn't hear any panicked screams from the inhabitants of the Island.

The absence of screams of horror was a cultivated development. Time and inventions had manipulated and dimmed the fears attached to the state of being trapped on an Island.

The word 'island' was no more associated with a slow, painful death due to thirst and starvation but with the words 'exotic getaway'. The century-old scenario of shipwrecked passengers, swimming for their life, traversing the remains of their artificial habitat and finding solace in the first sight of land was turned 180 degrees. People came to islands willingly now- on not only boats but furthermore on seaplanes.

Even the waves, the invincible weapon of ocean were blocked at the periphery by the boundary of corals on all the sides except a part where one slender branch of deep ocean with its deep blue stretched towards the beach. But human ingeniousness prevailed and marked by bright red floating balls, the danger area was roped away to warn any stray humans curious or foolish enough to test nature.

A stretch of white sandy beach encircled the island. If one ventured beyond the beach, there was the forest of palm trees, rising on the floating landscape, the only stable thing in this fragile ecosystem.

Three figures were visible on the beach. A woman wearing a red bikini was soaking up the sun. The movement of her hand as she raised a glass to her lips was apparent. She was relaxed and enjoying the sun and the wind. I couldn't help but picture her in a primitive time when she would have been horrified at her current situation and would have been hastily hunting for a long sturdy branch of wood to write SOS in the sand.

A blue beach umbrella provided shade to the two men. The taller one seemed to have gone to sleep while the shorter one was sitting still, propped up on the backrest, staring at the ocean.

I was having a difficult time believing what lay in my line of sight. The scene was ethereal and for a mortal to peep into this paradise- it felt like an intrusion. Everything surrounding me was larger than life itself. The perfect collision of the sky blue, deep blue and aquamarine blue was a treasure that should be hunted for years or even centuries before a mortal could step here.

I was encroaching upon a world my mind was incapable of appreciating- much like an astronaut might feel when he steps for the first time into space. How do you comprehend such beauty? How do you explain that something like this exists?

But this was reality, and I was standing on the deck of my private overwater villa, overlooking the southwest side of the property, the superior villa with spectacular view of sunset.

An infinity pool occupied the deck on my left. The tiles inside were the colour of the lagoon water. The pool water reflecting that blue looked as if it was directly pumped from the ocean. Only the smell of chlorine and soft ripples slithering on the surface made by the jets present underwater gave it away.

A staircase at the edge of the deck provided a route to the lagoon below. It was quite a competition as to what looked more inviting- the pool or the ocean.

On my right was outdoor furniture set complete with a sofa, two chairs and a glass-topped table.

Another villa lay on my left, but the view was blocked with a wall of wood. The wall was so tall that you were effectively in your own world, in your own bit of paradise.

'Exclusivity' was the selling point.

Six pristine villas were constructed when the Embassy resort first came into business. For the 'crème de la crème', these spectacular villas were upraised on wooden pillars as an extension of the main island. A single 4 feet wide boardwalk was the only conduit to land, and these awe-inspiring, man-made structures were truly overwater.

It would be misleading to call it my private villa. I am nothing but a personal assistant, a factotum, or if you ask me to be downright candid- a knockabout. Doing the menial work is part of the job description, but I have never had a problem enjoying life on crumbs and living it to the fullest. In fact, I consider it my solitary redeeming quality.

The sound of a chair scraping against the wooden floor made me turn around. I did so sighing silently. The drudge for the day begins!

Jeffrey Dale- my boss- was in the motion of sitting down. He was a small man, but his thinness in the extreme gave the illusion of him being tall. Only when one stood next to him, one appreciated the illusion and how much it compensated for his small stature. The white shirt he wore was ironed to perfection, and the grey hair was still wet from the shower.

"Good morning Mr Dale," I said.

"Get me coffee," He said, "And remove this newspaper, I have no interest in knowing the current affairs of Maldives." The wrinkles on his face came into sharper focus as his face contracted with annoyance. The newspaper landed on the floor with a dull thud.

I picked up the discarded newspaper and walked inside through the glass doors. You might wonder how I was maintaining my composure, but the reality was this was as normal for me as breathing.

But during such incidences, I am always reminded of the day my path crossed with that of Jeffrey Dale. The laugh that escapes from my chest is ironic.

The dictum 'college will pass in the blink of an eye, and the real-life will start' was spot-on for my life. College had been a dead-end for me. I was earning my bread and paying my rent by doing measly jobs. That's what I was doing at the fateful night when I exchanged one bad job for another.

I was at a high-class dinner party as a part-time waiter, when I overheard an old man saying he needed a personal assistant in good physical shape. I had jumped at the chance because all my eyes had seen was an old man. A little bit of keeping him company, doing shopping for him and paying his bills- how difficult could that be? And for the first time, I would have a regular paycheck.

The 24-year-old me was gloating by the time he finished overhearing the end of that conversation. I sealed the deal that night itself. It felt like a Godsend gift. Finally, I will have a steady job instead of doing something for hourly payments.

But in retrospect, Jeffrey Dale should have said 'in need of a personal assistant in good mental shape'. The reality was far from what my brain had envisioned. Constant badgering was a way of life now. Apathy to the feelings of another human being was the motto of my employer, and though it seemed inconceivable to me in my past life, I now understood that some men do things without rhyme or reason. Some men are just evil.

The black espresso coffee machine stood on a marble-top entry table. Next to the device was a dark wood box with a glass lid and dividers inside to segregate five different blends of coffee. The top of the pods had a label detailing the strength and flavour of that particular pod.

I chose a dark roast and inserted it into the compartment on the top of the machine. The machine would remove the label, and the coffee would come out as pure as the water from the untouched and unseen glaciers. One last thing had to be done before the machine was fully equipped to do its job. I pulled bottled water from the mini-fridge next to the table and poured half of it into the glass back of the machine.

Then the machine was ready to be fired up. I clicked the switch to the 'on' position.

Four coffee mugs were gracing the top of the mini-fridge, nestled inside a tray. I picked one up and placed it on the receiving end of the machine just in time.

The coffee mugs much like the marble on top of the entry table was of jade green colour, as was everything else in the room. We had checked in last night, and this villa was rightly called 'Jade'. The villa host had explained the significance of the name while giving us a mini-tour.

The names of the villa corresponded with the colour scheme of that particular villa. Everything was jade green; even the furniture was not spared. The upholstery, the cushions, the curtains and all those knick-knacks you can imagine were of jade green colour. Our bathrobes, towels and bedsheets were mercifully spared, and they were white. The colour co-ordination had worked out beautifully. It was monotonous and yet not bland. Everything was custom made, nothing but the best for the 'esteemed' guests.

The entry hallway led to two bedrooms on either side. I had, of course, been assigned the smaller one on the left. The hallway ended into a living room- with two jade green sofa facing each other and a television at the apex.

The living room opened up to the deck and to the immense ocean beyond. The west wall of the entire villa was made of glass. The bedrooms and the living room were designed to remind the guests at all times that they were not residing on land but on water.

The machine stopped spitting and wheezing. No matter how much humans try to minimize their work, most of the time, they end up doing more to clean up the mess of the machine. I dutifully cleaned the spilled drops before grabbing the steaming coffee cup.

Mr Dale was hunched over the outdoor table writing in his diary. The sleeves of his shirt were pushed above his elbow, and his shoulders collected the loose fabric, bunching it between his shoulder blades. His focus was absolute as he wrote hurriedly oblivious to my presence.

Oh, how I wished to read that diary! But the man never left it alone. The diary was with him at all times. It was pocket-size, and he always carried it with himself. Though Mr Dale had it with him at all times, he rarely wrote in it. Only occasionally he would bring it out, from its sanctuary and scribble in it.

But his hands reached for his pocket many times in a day, to reassure him of its presence. Why was he so afraid of losing it? What was he writing in it? A lot of people had personal diaries, but his paranoia was bewildering. And his paranoia fed my inner frenzy and my mission to read it.

Well, one day, he will get sloppy; one day, I will lay my hands on it.

I coughed lightly to alert him to my company. He closed the diary swiftly in response without looking up, and the diary was in his pocket in seconds.

"I will have coffee at breakfast," He said, getting up.

"Do you want me to check if the breakfast buffet is open?" I kept my voice as steady as possible, still holding the steaming coffee cup.

"It's 9.30 Reece. Before disturbing the receptionist with such dumb questions do look at the clock," He replied, baring his yellow teeth in a sneer and led the way out.

2

Six over-water villas mounted on pillars of wood emerging from the seawater below formed a crude circle. Three villas on the east were rightfully called 'Sunrise facing', and the three on the west were conveniently called 'Sunset facing'.

The one-storey structures were nothing short of mini-bungalows- complete with a porch on the front and bicycles for the guests. The triangular gable on their roofs gave them a regal air and added a faux second storey. A metallic plaque was nailed to the main door- inscribed with the name of the villa to help the guests find the right one. Like there were so many villas that a sane person might get confused and enter the wrong one. I rolled my eyes at the absurdity.

Boardwalk upstretched on bleached wooden columns connected the over-water mini-bungalows to each other and to the main island. It was wide enough for a golf cart to pass (on which we were transported last night to our villa).

Our villa 'Jade' was the last one on the sunset facing side.

The wind was forceful and incessant outside with no physical obstacle to break its intensity. It came in a constant gush but gratifying at the same time because already the temperature was closer to 35 than 30 degree Celsius. The white cap I was wearing was doing an excellent job to keep the heat out, but my feet enclosed in flip-flops were exposed, and the skin was starting to burn. Loafers would have been a better choice and some sunscreen.

The only sound was that of the ocean and the air ruffling our clothes. We were the lone people out and about, and we might as well have been the lone people alive in the world.

I was walking four steps behind Mr Dale. Of course, he was walking as slow as a boring Sunday. His white hair was flying wildly in the breeze, his insignificant stature highlighted against the expansive scenery.

Eventually, we reached the end of the boardwalk. A signpost displaying the name 'Olive' was pointing at the restaurant.

The restaurant was a hovering one-room structure located on the east side. A branch from the main boardwalk provided a path lined with flowers in low rectangular flower pots. The faded colour of the flowers emphasized the fakeness of the blossoms and no further room was left for doubt about their aliveness as we reached the entrance to the restaurant. The double glass doors were adorned with hanging pots of orchids- safe and sound in the shade, the delicate petals alive and bright in shelter.

The glass doors were wide open, and a female attendant was standing behind a tall host station in the foyer. It was a small rectangular space that lacked natural light, and it was inexplicably dark and cold. The wall behind the host station was lined ceiling to floor with wine bottles. Hidden lights illuminated alternate rows, and the place looked like it was ready for cocktail hour. But the burn on my skin and the sweat on my forehead was a reminder of the hour.

"Good morning Mr Dale and Mr Oberoi. Welcome to our breakfast buffet," She said, smiling. Obviously, they knew our names! The attendant ushered us in, and I blinked rapidly to get used to the blinding light, percolating in from every inch of the glass walls.

The restaurant was spectacular, to put it mildly. Designed in an octagon shape, four of the walls facing the ocean were made entirely of glass. The French windows were open to allow the sea breeze inside, and the soft white curtains were swirling to confirm the presence of the invisible entity. The French windows led to a balcony lined by the same faux flowers in rectangular pots. Beyond that, the vast ocean stretched for hundreds of kilometres.

The waves were delivering the music, and the tranquil calm was to be cherished instead of drowned down, and so there was no artificial music. This was not a cheap place, not a shack where they play loud, raunchy music. This was all about embracing nature and pushing you to be one with its beauty. Nature was respected here for we were literally at her mercy.

The attendant handed us over to our server.

"This way, please. My name is Golo," He said in a thick local accent and guided us to a table in the centre of the room.

Small four-sided tables were spaced out to take up the room. All of them were topped with a small transparent vase holding a single yellow rose. Only two tables were engaged; one seated a family of three- a man, a woman and a teenage boy sitting in the centre of the room on the table next to ours. The red bikini tied on the nape of the neck was peeking from under the white dress the woman was wearing, this was undoubtedly the family I had spotted earlier on the beach.

An old Indian couple was sitting on a table close to the ocean; both wearing over-sized dark sunglasses with a designer name written in crystal studs on the temple. They sat across from each other, not talking and gazing at the ocean. But as we sat down, the old man looked at us with curious eyes.

"An egg-white only omelette with two white bread-toasted and black coffee with milk on the side- and don't burn it," Mr Dale had the order out of his mouth before I could settle in the beige upholstered chair.

The server looked at me anxiously expecting a similar discourse.

"I will have something from the buffet," I said quickly. Mr Dale glared at me as I stood up, but what can he do? The breakfast was included in the rate, and I was not going to have egg whites and bread.

Anything you could imagine having for breakfast in any part of the world was at display. The progression started with American breakfast options- pancakes, crepes, waffles, sausages, an egg counter, sliced avocado, fried potatoes, and bacon. Transitioning into a fruit bar with local and exotic fruits, a big bowl of whipped cream, flavoured yoghurts, parfaits in small transparent cups, colourful juices in tall glass pitchers.

And then there was food that I had never seen or heard of before. There were green and orange colour dumplings in circular bamboo boxes. Next to it was something labelled hummus, with fried balls that looked like pakodas and a basket filled with triangle-shaped breads. And at the end, there were cupcakes, scones, muffins and ice cream. I was confident that if I had asked for Samosa or Aloo Parantha, they would have prepared it especially for me.

A chocolate chip muffin of gigantic proportions caught my eye, and I was examining it when the smell of floral perfume encircled my vicinity.

"My favourite as well," The speaker was the Indian woman.

"Yeah, they look delicious!" I laughed lightly, putting a muffin on my plate.

"Are you from India?" She asked, picking up a muffin as well. She was definitely Indian; her black hair was cut short, and it fell just above her ears. The hair had more white than black, and she had made no efforts to hide her age. Her perfume matched her outfit- the flower print top and white pants were utterly western, but the accent gave her away.

"No, London," I replied.

"Travelling with your parents?" She asked.

"No with my boss. I am a personal assistant," I didn't look that young.

"Of that man?" She asked, eyeballing Mr Dale.

"Yes."

"We are here celebrating our 40th wedding anniversary. This trip was a complete surprise. I was sitting day before yesterday in my drawing-room, and my husband walks in and passes me this envelope. And guess what was inside?" She said, beaming at her husband over my shoulder.

"Tell me," I said, acting dense.

"The plane tickets to Maldives!" She said giggling.

"New friend Anisha?" A voice resonated from behind me. The man was the most over the top dresser I had ever encountered and mind you I had been a serving staff in some very exotic parties. He was wearing a white suit, with a pink shirt and a silk mustard pocket square. All that was missing was a white hat over his wrinkled face, and he would have blended well as a member of the mafia, " I am Om Vyas."

"Nice to meet you, I am Reece," I said, shaking his well moisturized, rings encrusted hand.

"This place is a dreamland," He said fidgeting with his cuff.

"Yes, I was telling Reece about how you surprised me. Just two days ago I was sitting in Mumbai, looking at the traffic on marine drive, listening to the noise of cars and now here I am looking at this beautiful ocean and listening to the music of nature," Mrs Vyas said, " Reece, why don't you join us for dinner tonight? If your boss will allow," Mrs Vyas asked me. Her eyes were kind, but I wasn't sure if her words had meant to make me aware of my position or a genuine concern about my liberties as an assistant.

It didn't matter anyway; I was going to ignore her invitation.

"Boss? What does he do?" Om Vyas looked up curious.

"He is retired. Please excuse me. I think he is looking for me," I said, inching away.

I sat down with a solitary muffin balanced on the now at best semi-warm plate. In my annoyance at the unnecessary inquisition by the Vyases, it took me a moment to realize that Mr Dale was watching the table next to ours. Gawking at it with extreme concentration would be a better description.

"What are you both looking at?" The man from that table said in a loud voice, putting his fork down, "Do I have to teach you manners?" He was a large man, and his face and neck was turning a deep shade of red.

I had twisted in my seat to locate Mr Dale's point of interest, and the man had caught us both spying on him and his family.

"Norman! I am sorry for my husband's manners," The woman said, putting her hand on the man's forearm to calm him down, "Evelyn Miller, and this is Jason, our son," She said, smiling genially at me.

The husband and the son glared at the female figure in their life in pure exasperation. But their defeated looks suggested that they were overruled quite often.

"I am Reece, this is Mr Jeffrey Dale. We are sorry, actually," I said talking in response to her welcoming smile.

Norman Miller was wearing a yellow polo t-shirt and brown shorts. He was a large man with broad shoulders, but his face was plump, and Mr Dale's constant scrutiny was starting to make him sweat.

"You are from America?" Jeffrey Dale asked in a caustic tone.

"Yes. You as well?" Evelyn Miller was determined to be friendly to the obnoxious old man.

Jeffrey Dale didn't reply. The way he was looking at Norman Miller, it was evident he knew him in some way. But Norman's response was puzzling. He sat like a bird trapped in the eyes of a snake. His face that was red a few minutes ago was now turning pale, and beads of perspiration was rolling down his forehead.

"After you are done stuffing your face, get my laundry," Mr Dale barked at me and stood up, throwing his napkin on the table.

The waiter who was putting his toast tray down looked at him astonished. Even Jason Miller, who was dutifully eating his fried beans and ignoring all of us looked up.

"What's wrong with that man?" Evelyn asked me as Mr Dale went out of sight.

"Absolutely no manners. Jason stay away from him," Norman Miller had regained his composure and was now digging into his hash browns, a sour expression on his face.

"Old men and their quirks. He is like 65," I said feebly, my face coloured and from then on I concentrated on shoving the chocolate chip muffin down my throat.

3

In the three-quarters of an hour that I spent indoors, the Sun had risen swiftly. It was now showering bolls of heat on the boardwalk, the sand and the sea. My brown sunglasses were ill-equipped for blocking the blinding light, and I kept my head down as I left the restaurant.

The charm and tranquillity of this morning had made way for sheer frustration. Treated as a servant in private was a tad better than treated like one in public. Before this holiday, I had never ventured out with Mr Dale in public. The humiliation had been behind closed doors and therefore was not something I concerned myself with. I was made of strong bones. Pride and ego were unknown elements in my life, until now.

Now other people were present to witness the degradation, and it was making me feel like a second-class citizen. The Vyases and the Millers were never going to look at me in the same light as they looked at each other. Mr Dale had set a precedent. I was his servant and not his assistant.

This 'holiday' that I had imagined to be a reward for my tolerance of the whimsicalities of Mr Dale was turning into a continuation of the nightmare I was experiencing for the past 6 months.

The ideal scenario was to locate the housekeeping staff, implore them to pick up the dirty clothes and pass the rest of my day in relative splendour. The flip side was to return to the villa without any information on 'how to get your laundry done on this wretched island' and hear another lashing from devil incarnate.

Thinking of the latter, I increased my pace.

A small hut, no bigger than a broom cupboard was located midway between the first and the last villa on the sunset facing side. A buggy laden with white sheets in a bundle was parked outside. Hoping that this was the base for the housekeeping staff, I climbed the two steps leading up to the shack.

The room was dark, and the wooden walls were squared into inbuilt shelves, loaded with bedsheets, towels and blankets. A ceiling fan was whirling at a lazy speed and was making more noise than serving its purpose.

Hassan- our villa host was drinking from a cup and reading a newspaper propped up against the water jug. He was wearing the same clothes as last night, when he gave us the tour of the villa- a loose cream cotton shirt with a red collar and matching cotton pants. In any other part of the world, his attire would have been considered shabby, but here it was labelled relaxed.

I knocked once on the open door.

Hassan looked up bewildered; his black cup tilted to one side in his confusion- the tea almost spilling out.

"Sir, you only had to call. You should not walk to find help. Our service is world-famous. Did someone not answer the phone when you called?" He said all this in one breath, abandoning his cup down in the sink.

"Mr Dale has some items he wants to get cleaned," I said.

"I will send the housekeeper immediately to Jade. It will be a fast track order, Mr Oberoi- don't worry. And I will talk to the manager to make it complimentary. I am so sorry you had to walk all the way," He said, bowing his head.

"No, please don't do all that. Just send someone to collect it," I said. Mr Dale should pay every single penny from his pocket.

Before Hassan could reply, a voice spoke from behind me.

"Monsieur excusez moi. We need an extra set of bathrobe," A man with silver hair was the speaker. He was holding his right hand's index finger up to denote how many bathrobes he needed.

Hassan all but fainted at this new intrusion.

"I am so sorry, Monsieur," He faltered a little trying to pronounce the French word, "We pride ourselves over our service," He repeated, "I cannot excuse myself over this mistake. I should have known your daughter would need one as well. Please forgive me," He replied hyperventilating.

"Please, my friend, do not get so tense. It's a bathrobe," The man replied in an appealing accent and once again raising that index finger.

I followed the charismatic guest out, leaving Hassan to deal with his anxieties solo. The tall figure walked gracefully down the steps and joined his family standing outside.

For a second, I thought it was Evelyn Miller, standing with her back facing me. This woman had the same exact shade of brown hair with the same length of hair crowning her head. Even their height was identical. But when the woman turned to face her husband, all the resemblance was lost.

She had bangs that were covering her entire forehead, and the eyebrows were thick and arched. Though it was bright and sunny, she had opted for glossy red lips.

Her lips were in high contrast with the yellow fitted sundress tight around her body.

But what most struck me was the distinctly different energy that was emitting from her. Something about her face set my muscles taut in defence. Maybe it was because hers was the blackest of eyes I have seen, and the primitive instinct in me rose up and cautioned me. Her husband stood next to her with a tranquil expression on his face when many a man would have gritted their teeth and scuttled away in the opposite direction.

The daughter with jet-black hair was wearing blue denim shorts and a white tee, had inherited her mother's black eyes.

"Bonjour," The woman said, noticing me.

"Hello," I replied, raising my hand in acknowledgement, "I am Reece."

"Noemie, Estelle and Raphael Le Gall," The man gestured with his hands to his wife then to his daughter and lastly put a hand on his chest. It was such a funny thing to do, and I sniggered involuntarily.

The daughter stood precisely where she was, motionless and glaring at me much like Jason Miller had at breakfast. They both must be at around the same age; the complicated age when you by default hate everyone new you meet, particularly people who are older than you.

I was standing on the lower step of the housekeeper's room during the conversation, and the villa Jade was visible from my perch. The front-facing porch was vacant a moment ago and then in the next second Mr Dale had materialized on it from nowhere. I signalled to him that I was on my way back but he at once started his hike.

Apprehension settled over me like a layer of dust, and I knew my lousy morning was giving way to a worse afternoon. I swallowed loudly in fright, and Raphael Le Gall looked up at me curiously.

"Who is he?" Raphael asked, tilting his head slightly.

"My boss," I replied in a deflated voice as both Noemie and Estelle Le Gall raised their eyebrows at my answer.

"Making new friends Reece," Jeffrey Dale had arrived. For a man who always rubbed people the wrong way, he wasn't shy of socializing.

I introduced the French family, disheartened. I was hoping Mr Dale would spare me at least in front of some people on this island. And now Raphael would likewise think I am beneath him.

"What do you do for a living Mr Le Gall?" Mr Dale asked.

"Oh, I have the most stereotypical job in Paris. I manage two art galleries," Raphael replied, opening his palm to show two fingers. The over-use of his hands was fascinating. I have only ever seen toddlers do that. Children

25

don't trust themselves to know the correct word for the figure they want to relay, and hence, they use their fingers to make sure the older person gets the right number. And there was something childlike about the face of Raphael Le Gall: The light blue eyes were like that of a baby, bright and kind, and though his jawline was prominent, owing to his thin build, his face was naive.

My mood became light; maybe the innocence of Raphael Le Gall would prevent him from judging me based on my position. The opinion of Noemie Le Gall didn't matter.

"Have you always lived in France?" Mr Dale asked. I groaned internally. Trust Mr Dale to ask silly and irrelevant questions.

"Oui, lived in France all my life, and I wish to breathe my last breath in my beloved country," Raphael said, putting both his hands over his heart, "No place like home."

"You remind me of someone I knew a long time back in America," Mr Dale fixed his milky grey eyes on the poor man and his wife. Noemie had not said a word till now in Mr Dale's presence and deducing from her unfocused eyes, I was sure her mind had long left the present conversation.

What was Mr Dale playing at? He knew the Millers, and now he pretends to know Le Galls as well. If he was using this as a technique to socialize- he was failing outstandingly.

Raphael had meanwhile lighted a thin cigarette and was puffing at it lightly. He didn't seem to think that Mr Dale's reminisces required a verbal answer.

Estelle said something to her father in French, "Papa J'ai faim."

"Au revoir," Raphael said shortly to us, smiling and followed his wife and daughter to the restaurant.

4

A full moon graced the night sky, the round orb dangling above the island. The hazy silver stairway to heaven formed, sparkled in the black water. But no matter how powerful the moon was, burning to its bursting magnificence, it couldn't overcome the mingled darkness of the vast ocean and the dark sky. Separated during the day they had become one now. No horizon was discernible, and they ruled the night jointly as one supreme power.

Strolling on the boardwalk, I walked unhurriedly, taking in the new views around. Everything changes in the night and the light, carefree, luminous world had transformed into a restful one. The air was colder, but the breeze was as strong as it had been in the morning.

The most significant transformation was that of the sound of the ocean. What was music to the ears in the morning was now a reminder of my vulnerability in this place. There was nowhere to run and nowhere to hide. If the ocean decided to knock me out, it would be swift and merciless. I shook my head at the dark thoughts and focused on the taste of delicious food still lingering in my mouth.

The dinner had been exceptional. Mr Dale and I had eaten in the privacy of our villa. He had scarfed his food down and left me alone to enjoy my portion in peace. And what a treat it had been! The risotto with three types of mushroom and a generous amount of parmesan cheese in the dish; the butter-soft bread with extra butter on top and to finish it a melt in your mouth, four-layered tiramisu cake.

A golf cart was stationary outside the first villa on the sunset facing side. The metallic plaque on the front wall of the villa etched with the words 'Peridot' was lighted up. I could only conclude from their naming system, Peridot must be a shade of green, for I had never heard of it before.

Hassan acknowledged me as he grabbed a mid-size suitcase and a brown leather duffel bag from the back of the buggy. I had spoken more to him in the past 24 hours than anyone else, and his face had become familiar and comforting.

"Good evening sir. I hope you were happy with the laundry," He asked. The energy of the man was unending, and the dedication towards the Embassy resort was unshakeable.

"Yes, thank you for the fast service. Mr Dale was most grateful," I added a fib. Mr Dale had not even bothered to unpack the bundle of freshly laundered garments, "New guests?" I asked.

The lamp of the entry table was switched on inside the villa. The rest of the villa was in darkness- only the silhouette of a tall man was detectable. He was standing in the living room.

"One guest Sir and like many of the guests staying at our World-class resort, he's very famous," Hassan said in a boastful tone, his curly hair bouncing a little at his excitement.

"Where is he from?" I asked, curious.

"India, his name is Devin Langhar. He is very famous. But we are used to celebrities, and for us all our guests are celebrities," Hassan replied.

A famous person! He was sure to be an Indian actor. But I have never heard of the name before. I raked my memory for an actor or a musician named Devin Langhar. It was such an unusual name, hard to forget, but nothing came back to me.

"Did I tell you about the time Cristiano Ronaldo- the legendary footballer stayed at our resort?" Hassan added, filling his lungs with air and putting the suitcase down on the boardwalk.

"Gotta get some exercise- all this food!" I said hastily and made an escape before Hassan got a chance to utilize his lungful of air. I was not ready to be the best of friends, at least not yet.

Dim lights embedded in the wood, on either side of the boardwalk, illuminated the pathway. The restaurant was brimming with activity. The balcony was lined with tables, and the bright lights escaping from the open French windows were throwing golden streaks on the seawater below.

I chose the opposite side of the beach from the restaurant for the walk. It was quieter and darker, and in sync with my thoughts.

A wooden staircase was fixed at the side of the boardwalk, where it ended, leading to the beach down below. The boardwalk ended in a curve and continued, as a sandy path, leading up to the main island. At the end of the curve, though invisible from here, a guard sat trying to ensure that this part of the island remained exclusive.

I climbed down gradually; making sure my footing was foolproof. It was far darker here on the beach, and there were no man-made lights.

This was the first time I had stepped on a beach in my life if I don't count the one time I took a trip to Brighton with my mother and father. That beach was cold and damp, and we wore our heavy jackets throughout.

This Maldivian beach, in contrast, was the definition of an ideal beach. The air was warm, and the sand was cold. The fine powdery granules were reflecting the moonlight, and they shone ever so subtly, invisible, imperceptible and diminutive in comparison to the colossal scene around me but supremely beautiful in their own little universe.

The beach was littered with skeletons of corals and shells of departed marine life. Hoping they were departed from the mortal world, I removed my flip-flops to enjoy the coolness of the sand. It was not one of my brightest ideas. The spikey skeletons made the walk downright painful, it was like walking on pins and needles. In half a minute, I gave up and put my slippers back on.

The coastline was spindling, and I walked closer to the trees. Here in the shadow of the trees, the moonlight failed to penetrate, and it was pitch black. The ghostly shadows seemed to move as the breeze ruffled the towering foliage. I almost turned around for the safety of the villa and the human elements surrounding it. Still, my consciousness prevailed overriding my instinct, and I continued walking-the false bravado wanting to add a tale to my book of adventures.

The two reclining chairs at the end of my walk were sans cushion. I had walked for 10 minutes to reach the spot. After this point, the beach curved and went out of sight. I didn't have either motivation or courage to go that far in the darkness.

From here, I could see the Sunset facing villas, glowing on my right side, and I knew safety was within reach.

I should be enjoying and savouring every minute, but my instinct was on alert. I was scared more than excited. I was miserable more than happy. My subconsciousness was the North Pole and my consciousness the South Pole. They refused to exist together, pulling me apart and giving me a constant dull headache.

It was unquestionably something to do with the feeling of being trapped. This was unnatural. It was as bad as being on an aeroplane or a boat. One can't do anything about it, and you are at the mercy of other people and their actions. Only here I was at the mercy of nature.

And I was stuck here for 10 days, with Jeffrey Dale.

How long was I going to be able to do this job? I was perpetually in a state of misery. I was aware when I took the job that I would be serving coffee most of the time. Still, the humiliation, the constant reminder of my place was becoming intolerable, more so when there were so many people around me to witness the degradation.

But I cannot resign. I was sure that if I left this job voluntarily, knowing the callous nature of Jeffrey Dale, I was not going to get a letter of recommendation. And glowing references were vital in this field for who will hire a personal assistant without one.

I don't have to work forever for Mr Dale. I consoled myself. He was in his late 60s. Sooner or later, he will die, and that was the only consolation.

I was about to resume pacing when I heard footsteps in the forest and then all at once, a voice rang out without warning.

"I am not asking for something impossible," My jaw dropped reflexively as I recognized the voice of Mr Dale. Even though he was whispering, the raspy voice was still conspicuous.

The beach chairs were high back, but they were in a reclining position. I shifted my stance and lay as flat as possible so that the back of my head was not visible to the people in the forest.

"You are a man of means. You are holidaying here in this five-star resort. I am only asking you to help out a fellow man in need," Mr Dale said softly, " I am simply asking for a price to protect your secret. Think of it as you are paying the bank to keep your money safe. In this case, to protect your life from turning upside down."

"This is blackmail!" Another man's voice whispered back.

"Now you are making me angry using such ugly words. Take the night and think over the matter. I will speak to you again," Mr Dale said loudly, dropping all efforts to keep his voice low.

Two pairs of feet retreated into the woods, and all was quiet. I sat up straight slowly, trying to process the exchange I was obviously not meant to hear.

Blackmail! This caps everything malicious Jeffrey Dale has ever said and done. But to be honest, I wasn't really surprised. He fitted like a custom made Lego piece in the tower of the despicable humans who prey on other individuals.

The looming question was, who was the target? The man's voice had been quite soft. It had taken all my concentration to piece together his end of the conversation. I couldn't recognize his voice.

And we have been here one day. Had Mr Dale seen something or heard something worth blackmailing in a matter of 24 hours? The target must have some rotten luck.

My mind spun trying to recall all I had witnessed till now, and in a millisecond it zeroed in on the glaring contest between Norman Miller and Jeffrey Dale at breakfast today. Of course! There was obviously something suspicious in that interaction. The way the antagonism had developed so rapidly was absurd. The image of the red, sweating face of Norman Miller materialized in front of my eyes. I had assumed it to be a sign of Norman Miller's disposition. A lot of middle-aged men were short-tempered, but maybe his anger had been a façade to hide his terror. After all, offence is the best defence. Perhaps he thought that if he intimidates Mr Dale with his loud voice and wild words, Mr Dale would be cowed into backing off.

But the strategy had evidently failed, and Jeffrey Dale had cornered him in a matter of a few hours...

5

I was trapped in one of those states that happen in the early hours of the morning.

The air in the room is unnaturally cold, but you are sheltered from it. Your body has released heat for 8 hours during the night, and the heavy blanket has done an excellent job of retaining it.

You are lying flat on your bed, cosy but getting a jot impatient from being prostrate for so long. Your mind is between the state of being awake and being asleep. Your vision to the world is sealed; still, your mind is accurately projecting a picture of your surroundings behind your closed eyes. The projection is as real as the motion of your chest moving up and down with each breath you take.

The dream you were dreaming is finishing up in the background. You are not a part of that dream anymore, but you are polite and waiting for the last character to say its final words and leave the fluid stage.

Such was my state the next morning, when three rapid knocks intruded the silence. I lay without moving and waited for the person at the door to give up and leave. Sighing I hastily pulled the white terry dressing gown over my pyjamas as another knock resounded from beyond the foyer. The jade-green clock on the bedside table displayed 8.00am.

The door to Mr Dale's bedroom was closed, exactly as it had been last night. I had stumbled back late last night, hoping and praying he had retired to bed, and the wish had been fulfilled. To maintain a straight face, after the things I had overheard was akin to a herculean task for a for me and I was glad I didn't have to come face to face with that man.

I opened the door to find the manager of the resort standing outside.

"Excuse me for encroaching upon your privacy early in the morning. I am Mark Nettles- the manager of Embassy resort. May I come in?" He said and walked right in without waiting for me to give an affirmation.

"Yes, I met you on the day we checked in. What's up?" I asked whispering.

Mr Nettles was dressed in a light blue linen shirt and a pair of white shorts. The shirt clung to his big belly and emphasized it. His relatively thin legs ended in feet enclosed in beige loafers. If he had not told me his designation, I would have mistaken him for one of the guests.

"Where is Mr Dale? I need both of you," He said, looking around and not taking the trouble to keep his voice down. For a person in the hospitality business, this middle-aged man surely was too imposing.

"I will rouse him if there's the need for it. What's this about?" I asked flatly.

"There was rather an unfortunate incident last night. Now I don't want you to panic. We are doing everything and beefing up the security," He said, " Please enjoy your vacation in peace. Incidents like these are uncommon."

"But what happened?" I asked again.

"The villa across from yours was robbed," He gestured in the direction of the alleged villa.

"What? Was anyone hurt?" I asked taken aback at the extraordinary incident. Robbery! It's common in hotels with hundreds of rooms but for a theft to occur in a resort with 6 villas. How often does that happen?

But then again I did witness a blackmailing last night; maybe it was not extraordinary at all. Perhaps things like this are typical on an Island. The sarcasm in my head was real, but so was the fear. What was Mr Dale up to?

"Thankfully, everyone is safe. But some prescription medicine was stolen. Did you see anything at all?" Mr Nettles asked.

"No. What time did it happen?" I asked, thinking back to last night. I was back at the villa by 10.45pm; everything appeared peaceful around me till that time.

"We are not sure yet but possibly late at night, after 11.00pm, when the family had gone to bed. Will you please get Mr Dale? I need to ask him the same questions. Every input is important," He said, nodding towards the closed door.

It would be illuminating to see Mr Dale's face when the manager asked the questions. How much or how well will he be able to hide?

"Wait here," I said and knocked lightly on the door, "Sir, are you awake?"

I opened the door, getting no response, but the room was vacant. The bed was slept in, and one pillow was on the floor. The air conditioning was switched off, and the curtains were open. Crossing the room, I entered the dressing area, and then checked the bathroom. But there was no one there.

"Maybe he has gone for a walk," I suggested.

"Please contact me or any hotel staff if you remember anything."

"Whose villa was it?" I asked following him out.

"The Millers- they are from America. This has never happened in any of our resorts! The management is going to take strict measures that something like this never reoccurs in the future. Still, I would urge all our guests to be extra cautious with their belongings. The resort cannot be held responsible for any lost or stolen property. Please use the safe provided in your villas. And lock the doors- both front and back- if you leave the villa and during the night before you go to sleep," Mark Nettles parroted out the guidebook he would have memorized once upon a time, "Excuse me I need to talk to other guests," He said and walked towards the Vyases villa next door.

The utterly bizarre events of last night- the blackmail and the robbery, they have to be connected somehow. What were the odds that a theft and blackmail would take place during the same night in such a small geographical area? And what are the odds that Norman Miller is in the eye of both the storms?

I glanced at the burglarized villa across. It was devoid of any activity and the morning looked as calm and as bright as the one yesterday. Yet a robbery and blackmail had taken place in this apparent paradise within the space of a few hours.

A movement in the periphery caught my attention. A tall figure was standing at the convergence point of sunset and sunrise branches of boardwalk, facing the ocean. I had merely caught a glimpse of the illustrious guest from the villa 'Peridot' last night, but the tall, lanky build was distinct. Taking advantage of the situation, I marched forward to introduce myself. It always helps knowing famous people.

"Good morning," I said brightly.

The famous guest whipped his head in surprise, and I felt a trifle embarrassed. I had broken into his reverie, and the startled brown eyes shifted from confused to contemplating in a second. My attire was contributing to my embarrassment. In my haste, I had padded out wearing the dressing gown and the bathroom slippers.

The man gave me a look over, his face pensive, as if he hadn't made up his mind about me. The face was unknown to me, however.

He was easily 6 feet tall. I placed him to be in his late 30s or early 40s. His face was narrow but ended in a sharp jaw. The lips were thin and looked thinner due to his current meditating expression.

"Did you hear about the robbery?" I asked when he didn't reply.

"Yes. Mr Nettles was here a few minutes ago. I am Devin Langhar," He replied. His voice was low, and his English had a trace of Indian accent.

I thought through the list of all the famous people I knew but came up short. He didn't look like an actor or a musician anyways.

"Reece Oberoi. Forgive me for this intrusion, but I was curious. Hassan gave the 101 yesterday- that you were this famous man from India," I said.

"That's not 101," He replied, raising his eyebrows imperceptibly. He didn't smile. The ruminating expression was still in place.

"So what field are you famous in?" I prompted.

"I am a professor of criminal psychology," Mr Langhar replied.

"And you are famous?" My tone must have seemed more incredulous than the words for he laughed out loud.

"In some circles," He replied.

I didn't know how to respond to that. Mr Langhar was a man of limited words, and there was only so much I could say without coming across as an idiot.

"I have to get back. It was nice to meet you," I said. Mr Langhar gave me a tight smile in reply.

He seemed like an ordinary man, and I wondered if Hassan was mistaken about his fame. Why would a professor of criminology be famous?

6

An hour later, I strolled in for breakfast. I was showered, dressed and in the company of Mr Dale. The restaurant 'Olive' had changed its layout significantly overnight. Individual tables were now joined together to form one large table in the centre of the room.

Judging by the glowering of the wait staff, standing idle near the entrance, the new arrangement was certainly made against the wishes of the management.

Mr Vyas motioned to two open seats next to him as we walked in. I was sceptical regarding Mr Dale's mood, but he started towards the table before I got a chance to say anything and took the vacant chair next to Om Vyas.

Everyone likes gossip, I guess.

I slid into the last available chair, and the group was complete. Evelyn and Norman Miller were sitting at the head of the conference table, the ocean forming the backdrop. Next to them on the left were the Vyases and then Mr Dale and I. On my left was a couple I had yet not met. I nodded at Mr Langhar, seated across from me. The circle ended with Le Gall's sitting on the right of the Millers.

"We slept through the whole thing. You would think that with such a dangerous person lurking in our villa we would have some premonition!" Mrs Miller resumed her speech, "Especially I being a mother- but no, I slept like a baby the entire night," Her eyes were wide, and her hands rested weakly on her lap, the gold band glowing lightly on her left ring finger.

"Very horrible thing to happen anywhere but for a robbery to happen in this place. A five-star resort! We paid so much money. The least they can do is assure us of our safety," Mrs Vyas said, leaning forward, her wrinkled face alarmed, "At least nothing seriously bad happen," She patted Mrs Miller on the shoulder.

"Believe me, Mrs Vyas, I have thanked our stars a thousand times since this morning. Jason- our son- was sleeping in the next room alone! God forbid if the monster was not satisfied with what he found and wanted more," Evelyn looked up to her son. Jason was standing against the pillar behind his parents. The teenager's arrogance was subdued today, but he looked bored.

"And what if one of us had woken up. Now I am glad we didn't wake up and interrupt his search," Mrs Miller covered her eyes with her hands. Mrs Vyas patted her shoulder once again.

"Do you know the time all this happened?" The woman sitting next to me asked. Her accent was Indian. She looked young at first glance, but on closer inspection, I put her close to 40.

"No, Mrs Kumar. We were fast asleep. We noticed it in the morning and alerted the manager," Mr Miller replied.

"What did they take?" The man sitting on her side asked who was probably Mr Kumar.

"My anti-anxiety medicine," Norman replied, his pale complexion turning pink. The attitude change of Norman Miller was surprising. Yesterday he had been furious about something as simple as being gawked at, and then there was his attitude today. There had been a robbery in his villa. Contrary to being angry and yelling, here he was unsure and scared. There were dark circles under his eyes, and he looked as if he had a sleepless night. But that was not possible, for Evelyn told us a moment ago that they had slept through the entire night- like a baby.

I looked at Mr Dale sitting next to me- quiet and observing. His eyes were on Norman Miller; watching his prey, the trap already set, counting the minutes to his reward.

"He must be an addict- a junkie," Raphael said.

"Norman, I also suffer from anxiety, and I have a prescription. I would be happy to lend you some tablets," Om Vyas said.

"I will be fine," Norman Miller replied.

"Are you going to call the police?" Mr Dale asked. What an odd question to ask? Everyone around the table had shown sympathy for the Millers, but Mr Dale was more concerned with the police. If there was any doubt left in my mind, it was all wiped away like chalk from a blackboard! Jeffrey Dale did blackmail Norman Miller last night!

"I doubt they will be able to catch the culprit with so little to go on. We didn't see or hear anything. Besides this is our holiday- we don't want to completely ruin it," Evelyn replied.

"You will let them get away? But Norman, Evelyn- criminals should be caught and punished," Mr Vyas said indignantly.

"You would be surprised to know Mr Vyas how many people get away with crime. Serious crimes," Mr Dale leaned forward, fixing his gaze once more on Norman Miller.

There was utter silence after Jeffrey Dale's statement.

"This is a petty crime- there's no need to be so dramatic, Mr Dale," Evelyn laughed at his expression. But her body's reaction and her tone were out of sync. She reached out for her husband precisely like she had yesterday morning and gripped his arm.

"You were crying a minute ago, Evelyn. A petty crime can lead to a serious crime. You don't know what this thief has in mind- maybe he will get bold. It's only robbery you say- and tomorrow it will only be murder," Mr Dale's voice rang with menace.

Everyone in the room shivered at the last word, at least I did. Blackmail and robbery was one thing but murder!

"It sounds as if you know a lot about crimes and murders," Mr Kumar said, eyeing Mr Dale with suspicion.

"I was in the newspaper business for three decades and an investigative journalist in my younger days. The things I have seen and known and remembered," Mr Dale hissed the last word out, "Crimes that go unpunished have always been fascinating. The satisfaction of seeing a person squirm, when I am in on the secret; to know the extent of the crime- to see the fear in the eyes, the haunted look, that they really can't escape their fate after all. That someone has seen them do it and know their truth," He stopped short in his sentence as if he remembered where he was all of a sudden, "All I want to say is you should not

44

ignore a crime," He finished his sentence hastily, but the damage was done.

"I have told them to install cameras outside the villas..." Mrs Miller picked up the conversation after a minute of silence, but I zoned out from the discussion.

Mr Dale's face was arrogant, and his eyes were sharp and bright. I could sense his brain spinning a web, and I wondered what Norman Miller had in store for today and would he survive another storm?

The past had long arms, and it was going to catch up with him, aided by Jeffrey Dale.

7

The 'breakfast group' disbanded speedily following the reckless statements of my boss. And I was alone now, to relish a scrumptious plate of scrambled eggs with cheddar cheese, a stack of chocolate chip pancakes and to complete the calorie dump- an Irish coffee.

I ate slowly, organizing my thoughts and observations, the sea breeze wafting in delicately like a faint scent from incense lighted in the other room.

Mr Dale had been the first person to abandon the table. He had left without saying goodbye to other guests and for once, not giving me any orders.

The breath of relief taken in by Norman Miller after Jeffrey Dale left was loud, and confusing for some guests around the informal conference table.

But his wife and I did not react. Norman Miller' s sigh of relief was an expected sign for us.

An odd person to add to this short list was Devin Langhar. He like us was not baffled at the obvious sign of release from Norman Miller. And that was odd, if not the most peculiar thing I had witnessed in this illusion of a paradise.

Devin Langhar had not spoken a single word throughout breakfast. And yet he had picked up the antagonism between Norman and Mr Dale. How was he able to read the room so quickly? And he had not shown any curiosity. Mr Langhar had looked bored as he sat there, listening to the conversation. Whether it was due to the absence of a curious mind or from the confidence of comprehending everything that needs to be comprehended in a flash, I cannot say.

Devin Langhar had been nonchalant about his profession, but now I wondered whether that was on purpose. Mr Langhar had me intrigued almost as much as the whole business between Jeffrey Dale and Norman Miller.

Forty-five minutes later, I was back at the villa.

A small piece of paper was lying flat on the entry table. It was from Mr Dale notifying me that he was at the spa.

Immediately I felt like I was a kid in a candy store. I can finally enjoy the numerous amenities of the villa 'Jade' without the constant supervision of my boss. But that was not the only good piece of news waiting for me at the villa.

A glass dish laden with the most beautiful teacakes was also gracing the entry table. The bite-size teacakes were arranged in a row of 4 down and across, protected with cellophane and complete with a jade green flower on top.

A jade envelope was propped up against the coffee maker. My name was at the top alongside that of Mr Dale, so I didn't have second thoughts about slitting it open. Inside was a single piece of paper reading,

Dear Mr Dale and Mr Oberoi,

Let me take this opportunity to thank you for choosing the Embassy Resort for your vacation. We always strive to give you the best holiday experience. With that in mind, our management team has designed a special evening just for you

and the guests in the adjoining villas at the boathouse club tonight.

We look forward to an evening with you from 7.00pm onwards.

Dress code-casual.

Thanking you,

Mark Nettles

(General Manager)

P.S. Please find the map to the boathouse on the other side of this leaflet.

I replaced the letter in the envelope and kept it precisely in the same place.

The motives of Mark Nettles, the manager of the resort was clear. The reputation of the resort had to be restored. He must have gotten a hint that the Millers had discussed their grievances in public today. And he came up with a party to appease the guests. It was sort of like putting duct tape on a sinking boat, but it might work if the hole is small. And the temper of exclusive guests is unpredictable, after all.

I yawned loudly. Of all the things I could have done, from enjoying a hot cup of coffee with the option of choosing from a million types of roast to using the private swimming pool or lying on the swing bed on the deck and gaze at the colourful ocean, a nap surpassed all the other alternatives.

I hastily discarded my t-shirt at the foot end of the bed. The belt followed the t-shirt, and I opened the top button of my jeans to give my waist some room to breathe, too lethargic to pull it down all the way. I pushed a button on the side of the bedside table, and dark curtains descended, making a pleasant humming sound to block the ever-present sunlight. The linen comforter felt like clouds on my skin, shielding me from the cold air conditioning. My eyelids grew heavy, and it was like I hadn't slept for days. I heard someone open the door of the villa, but I was too far gone to get up to check.

Besides, who knew if it was a part of my dream or an event from my reality?

8

The queen-size bed was littered with the full contents of my suitcase- a white shirt, 2 pairs of jeans, 5 T-shirts, including my only black Ralph Lauren polo t-shirt. Mercifully I had the foresight to pack a plain black jacket. Though the invitation mentioned no dress code, my sixth sense was impressing upon me- it was a trick, and I would be a fool to underdress and go in shorts and a white t-shirt.

I ended up choosing the Ralph Lauren polo, black jeans and the black jacket. *When in doubt, go all black.* My black hair was whipped into submission by hair gel, and I artfully let a couple of strands fall on my forehead. A generous spritz of the cologne completed the attire for the evening.

Mr Dale's bedroom door was ajar, and I peeked inside. It was uninhabited like this morning. I tiptoed inside, suspicious if he was in the bathroom. But the shower and the dressing area were uninhabited as well. This was the time to seize the day, and I crossed the room in long strides. The bedside table drawer only fetched me his mobile phone and his insulin injections. There was no sign of the mysterious black diary. Same disappointment met me when I opened the work desk drawer.

I was scared to fidget with the suitcases lest I disturb the arrangement. Besides I was sure, Mr Dale would not keep his cherished possession there, for anyone to find.

The cellophane sheet lay discarded on the entry table, and two of the teacakes were missing. The invitation letter was lying outside its envelope, squished and transformed into a ball. I put the letter and the envelope in the dustbin.

Then pulled the cellophane cover back on the cake platter, grabbing a mini vanilla and chocolate-layered cake with an edible gold leaf on top. I balanced the dish inside the mini-fridge and ate the cake in a bite at the same time. *Why don't things taste as good as they look?* I drank half a glass of water to remove the dry taste from my mouth. It was like biting into a sponge made for scrubbing dishes.

I locked the front door remembering the cautionary words of the manager. I was too uncaring to check the backdoor, leading inside from the swimming pool. I didn't have anything worth stealing, and I was indifferent about the belongings of Mr Dale. It would actually be a humbling experience for him if a theft happened again tonight.

The housekeeping cabana was the only one with some activity, and Hassan poked his head out as I walked past it.

"Have a good evening, Sir," He said, his face cheery.

A woman was with him inside. She was wearing the same trousers and shirt as Hassan. Hassan's eyes were watching her, and then he said in a loud voice-

"No, Bhakti! You fold it like this," He snatched the towel the woman was folding and proceeded to show her and me the correct way.

"There are many ways to fold a towel, Hassan," Bhakti snapped back. Her voice was nasal, and she rolled her eyes, turning her head towards me- like I was supposed to side with her.

"Yes but this is the right method. Bhakti, you are late. Take the wine to the party now. You are going to love the red wine chosen for tonight's party, Sir," He said to me, "It's vintage wine."

Hassan dropped to his knees to retrieve the wine crate.

"Where is it?" He asked, still down on the floor, looking at the empty space under the counter.

"Hassan that's why you should listen to me. It's wine- I put it in the fridge," Bhakti said, again looking at me and swelling at her brilliance.

Hassan rose slowly like a snake but without rage, too shocked to show his wrath.

"You put the vintage red wine in the fridge?" He asked in a small voice.

"Yes, it's served cold!" Bhakti shook her head, her plump body shaking with laughter.

"I need to get going," I said coughing delicately sincerely hoping they both still have jobs this time tomorrow, at least Hassan.

The sun was lingering over the horizon, at the cusp of making its journey to jumpstart the day for people in the other half of the world. The moon was on the other side, prepared to take over the obligations on this half. The warm breeze was strong, but the hair gel was doing its job adequately, and I walked carefree towards the destination.

I retraced my steps from last night- the same wooden staircase leading to the beige beach below, the same powdery fine sand littered with millions of shells. But now in the comfort of daylight, it looked inviting and heavenly.

Was it only yesterday that I had sauntered this same path, obsessing over the state of my affairs and at the end of the evening, walked back to the villa in a dazed state? Was it only today that the manager had knocked on the villa door? The blackmail and the robbery seemed like something that happened a long time ago- an anomaly in any case.

Today all I wanted to do was have a good time without worry, and Mr Nettles was going to ensure it.

The map to the boathouse took me beyond the curve of the beach, beyond the beach chairs of last night. The curve straightened and stretched into a beach with similar landscape- a forest of palm trees on one side and the lagoon water on the other.

A small structure obstructed the horizon, and the setting sun was hidden behind it. The boathouse was half the size of the restaurant. Like everything else, it was made of wood and sitting on wooden pillars. The roof was rectangular, the eaves lined with golden string lights, twinkling in the twilight.

Six red kayaks tied under the boathouse were hovering over the gentle waves, blundering into each other with timed perfection. But the dull thud created was masked by the music coming from inside.

The platform leading up to the boathouse began on the beach and arched, forming a small bridge to lead inside. Oil-filled lamps residing in glass jars lined both sides of the boardwalk. Within a few minutes, they would be sparkling alongside the stars.

A man was standing in the middle of the bridge, holding a champagne glass.

"Good evening Reece," Om Vyas acknowledged me. Of course, the peacock man was wearing a full suit, a brown coat with checks all over.

"Hello. Nice jacket," I added perfunctorily.

"Thank you. It's an anniversary present from my wife," He touched his lapel, hoping I would notice the logo in the form of a gold lapel pin. *Why would he want to impress someone as underprivileged as me?*

"She forced me to take this vacation. I am always busy with work and no time to play or dress up," He continued, "Did I tell you about my business?"

"No," I replied.

"I own a car parts business. There's a lot of money but no time to rest. But I have made my fortune from nothing; build my business from the ground up. I came to Bombay when I was a young man of 21 years! Not a rupee in my pocket, not a cloth to my name. And now look at me," He said, his eyes bright, and he raised his champagne glass to salute himself.

"Yes, your hard work has paid off," I replied and then said hurriedly before he could tell more anecdotes, "Shall we?"

"I will come with you," He said, ignoring my tone and drained his glass dry.

Mark Nettles, the manager was at the entrance greeting newcomers with a handshake, very much like a Priest welcomes his parish members when they come to church on a Sunday morning.

"Welcome Reece and welcome again, Mr Vyas," He laughed out loud and shook my hand. His outfit was as bizarre as that of Om Vyas- a white coat and a white shirt inside with a metallic green tie. Was there a special fashion magazine for men of their age? Perhaps a magazine article called- how to stand out in a party, fail-proof ways! The cringe fashion was bewildering.

A waiter materialized in front of us holding a tray laden with sparkling champagne- the bubbles rising from the bottom of the thin, delicate glasses as a fast-moving stream. Om Vyas and I took a glass each obliging him.

The boathouse was half the size of the restaurant but still adequate for the number of people present. A stage was set against the west wall, and four round tables were grouped around it.

The west wall, without a doubt, was the most treasured in this resort and consequently, it was made entirely of glass- showing us the full breadth of ocean. The sky illuminated with the pink, and orange glow left after sunset, was acting as the backdrop. The exposed logs of woods added character to the walls.

A miniature low stage was crowded with a small band. The four members of the group were shrouded in semi-darkness, the natural backdrop casting long shadows on their face but the youngness of their face was still perceptible. They were playing the kind of music that could be enjoyed or ignored. It was loud enough to grasp and low enough for one to have a proper conversation without shouting in his or her companion's ears.

Mr Dale was sitting at a table close to the bar, sharing it with Mrs Vyas. Mrs Vyas was in causal attire- wearing beige pants, a loose white full sleeve top and a single heavy gold chain around her neck.

"Good evening," I greeted them both. There was assigned seating and my name printed on a card was kept on the table.

"Good evening Reece. Thank you for bringing my husband back," Mrs Vyas chided her husband as he sat down next to her, "He has a habit of running away."

"Trust me, Anisha. I am not going to run away after so many years of marriage," Mr Vyas said, giving her a slight peck on the cheek.

I don't know why I was the one who blushed, but I turned my head in embarrassment and caught Mr Dale scowling at me.

"The magazine I was reading at the airport- for some reason it's not in my room. I have told you countless times not to touch my things without asking me first," He raised a finger in warning as I opened my mouth to defend myself, "I don't care what you did, why you did. I want that magazine tomorrow at breakfast with my coffee."

"Yes Sir," I replied, real embarrassment colouring my face, and the back of my neck started to burn.

A scoff was the response to my polite statement. The Vyases were looking anywhere but at me. The table on our left was assigned to the Millers and Le Galls, and it was evident they had overheard my humiliation as well.

Luckily a loud clearing of throat resounded from the surround sound system. Mark Nettles was hovering over the microphone. He seemed to be standing a little straighter than his usual posture. I welcomed the sudden distraction.

Hopefully one could count on the short-term memory of people, and I will be granted the wish of passing this promising evening incognito.

9

The glass wall behind the stage was nothing but a black mirror now. The vicinity of the microphone was alight due to a spotlight, and Mr Nettles' white coat radiated like moonstone in the brightness as he adjusted the microphone stand to his height.

The rest of the room was obscured in semi-darkness. Whatever faint light was there, it was coming from sconces attached at the back wall, near the entrance.

The scene thus set, the manager of Embassy resort began speaking-

"Ladies and Gentlemen, let me welcome each and every one of you," Opening his arms as wide as they would go he said, "We always try to put this beautiful boathouse ...don't you agree it's stunning! I have always been a fan of rustic charm. We always try to put this beautiful boathouse to good use. And what better use than to entertain our most esteemed guests, the most important people at this resort," Mark Nettles raised his champagne glass to the audience.

He looked absolutely ridiculous wearing that white coat, looking dumpier if at all possible. I sent a wish to heavens that he won't start sweating or this could turn ugly. Om Vyas looked like a runaway model compared to him. But the manager was not done, and he put the glass down by his side and resumed-

"Mr and Mrs Miller I do want to formally apologize for the ordeal of last night. I sincerely hope that this beautiful evening we have planned especially for you will make up for the terrible inconvenience you had to endure. The lads from Maldives are here to give you company the entire evening, our upcoming local band," Mr Nettles signalled to the band in the background. The guitar player raised his right hand feebly to acknowledge the absent applause, "And we have a unique performance lined up for tonight. I am not going to elucidate on that or I will end up giving away the surprise. Please enjoy this evening, and I will be here the entire time to make sure that you all have a good time," He gave a silly little chuckle at the end and moved his pompous figure down.

I couldn't believe this guy was Australian. For some reason, I always pictured Australian people to be athletic, surfing, chiselled jawline and not the specimen that was presented to me here in Maldives.

"What an outstanding coat! I have to ask Mark where he got it," Mr Vyas said, "You know he personally came to our villa this morning, to inform us of the robbery."

"You were not singled out Mr Vyas. He went to everyone's villa," Mr Dale said in a falsely sweet voice.

How did he know? He wasn't even in the villa this morning.

Mr Dale had stumbled in as I was preparing to leave for breakfast and tagged along. I didn't have the bravado to ask him where he was though. I debated whether to confront him as to how he knew that Mr Nettles was in our villa, but then I didn't really care. It wasn't worth the degrading comments he was sure to fling my way.

The quartet band had resumed playing, and not a single person in the room was paying any attention to them. The band members were in turn not making eye contact with anyone. Their music was good but without any theatrics and they looked like teenage boys for whom playing music is everything. I looked at the band for a while out of politeness, but the performance was so spiritless, and my eyes began to wander.

The table on our right was dedicated to the kids if I could call them kids. Jason and Estelle were sitting there-looking at their phones. They could pass for brother and sister or near related cousins. Both had dark hair and were extremely skinny- all knees and elbows, as if they had their growth spurt this past month and the muscles were yet to catch up with the bones. The permanent scowl on their faces also contributed to the likeness.

The table on our immediate left was missing one person. Raphael had waived table service and was now at the bar.

Mr and Mrs Miller were sitting next to each other, and Noemie Le Gall was preoccupied with her compact mirror. The table on the far left was assigned to Devin Langhar and Mr and Mrs Kumar.

Already bored, I asked Mr Dale if he wanted something from the bar as an excuse to get up and stretch my legs.

"Get me an old-fashioned. Tip the waiter and tell him to use the best bourbon he has," He barked the order at me.

I rolled my eyes and got up.

A small bar was next to the stage, tucked away in the right corner. A solitary bartender was handling the blood alcohol level of the guests.

I am always amused at the way bartenders manage to keep themselves busy, and this one was no different. They will be either mixing the drink or rinsing a glass or chopping lemons, wiping the counter, arranging the paper napkins- you never see any bartender be still.

Raphael Le Gall balanced precariously on the high stool, with one long limb firmly on the floor, was slowly puffing away his thin cigarette. He was wearing a bizarre polo t-shirt with an intricate, to the point of optical illusion pattern in the front and a solid brown colour at the back.

"Are you allowed to do that?" I asked sceptically, pointing at the cigarette.

"I don't see a sign prohibiting me," He replied, chuckling.

"A beer and an old-fashioned please," I added to the waiter, interrupting his muddling of mint leaves.

"It was a nice thing for Mr Nettles to organize this party. He must be scared of losing his customers," Raphael said. His English was enchanting.

"I doubt he is going to redeem himself in the eyes of Mr and Mrs Miller," I said.

"Speaking of which..." He said and clammed up.

"Oh, Reece- are you enjoying the party?" Evelyn Miller joined us at the bar, "Hello again, Raphael."

"Yeah, the band sounds good," I replied, "What can I get for you, Mrs Miller?"

"Oh, thank you. It's always good to encounter a young man with good manners," She batted her eyes at me, "White wine please, whatever is open. I am not particular,"

She was dressed in an oversized white shirt, clinched at her waist with the help of a silver belt and black jeans. She looked beautiful now that she had put some colour on her face, and her bright pink lips pouted now and then.

"I hope you are feeling better now."

"Yes, thank you."

"And how is Mr Miller coping without his pills?" I said curiously.

"Oh, he will be fine. He only takes them when he has a mountain of anxiety. Luckily this is such a beautiful place that he can get distracted and not worry. We are going to try some water sports tomorrow- scuba diving and Jason is excited to do paddle boarding."

"He didn't look in the best of health this morning," I prodded.

"Oh, did you expect him to look good? He is a softhearted person. It's a robbery Reece, it could have turned easily into something awful," She smiled at me tightly.

Evelyn Miller knew about the blackmailing, of that I was sure. Otherwise, her restraint was inexplicable. I pinned her for a type of woman who loves attention and loves to drag and milk the topic that gives her attention to full capacity. And here she was tight-lipped and wanting to put the matter at rest.

Whatever Mr Dale had on Norman Miller must be significant; too big for idle gossip!

The bartender placed our drinks at the counter.

"Where are you going?" She asked pouting again as I started to walk away.

"I have to give this to Mr Dale," I pointed at the old-fashioned. She fumed for a millisecond and then turned her attention to Raphael.

"One old-fashioned," I said lightly.

"Reece, your work ethic is commendable. I am ready to hire a personal assistant myself. But only if he or she works as hard as you," Mr Vyas said, winking at me.

"You need to have enough money to afford one! And have enough money to not sweat when the personal assistant is lazy, and you are paying him more than he deserves," Mr Dale said, eyeing me viciously.

"We are both vacationing here, Mr Dale, in this five-star resort. This party is for the benefit of both of us," Om Vyas said, his voice going higher in volume.

Though it was fun to see two rich people fight, I spotted an open seat next to Mr Langhar and excused myself, leaving Mrs Vyas to be the moderator.

"Good evening Mr Langhar," I said.

"Good evening. Please sit Reece," Mr Langhar motioned at the vacant chair next to him. He was wearing a dark blue coat with a crisp white shirt, but his lapel pin was the most intriguing. It was in the shape of a thin arrow, made out of a bluish-purple gemstone.

Mr Langhar looked in a more accommodating mood this evening, "This is Ira and Shyam Kumar, Reece Oberoi," He made the introductions as I sat down.

"Were you named after that chocolate? The peanut buttercup thing?" Shyam asked chuckling.

"Good one," I forced a laugh, like I haven't heard that one before, "Are you from India as well?"

"We live in Dubai," Ira replied, putting a long-nailed hand under her chin. She had eyebrows so straight it was as if she had drawn them using a ruler. Her lips were thin in the extreme. Combined with the over the top spiky nails her appearance was that of a perpetually pissed off person.

"Never been there. What do you do?" I asked politely. I didn't particularly want to have a conversation with the duo from Dubai, but my other option was to go back and be the personal waiter of Mr Dale and perhaps Om Vyas as well.

"We have a family business. We provide soaps, shampoos- the whole caboodle to resorts and hotels," Shyam said.

"Including this one," Ira added, clinking her 3-carat diamond ring against her wine glass. For some reason, her husband threw her a furtive glance. It seemed like he was trying to caution her.

"That's fascinating. You should tell me more about it sometime," I said.

"Yes," Shyam said in a tone that made it clear that it was never going to happen, "We will get something to drink," Shyam added and left the table with his wife.

"At least Mr Vyas is not obnoxious," I muttered.

Mr Langhar raised an eyebrow, and his thin mouth stretched a little on one side.

"Where do you live in India, Mr Langhar?" I asked.

"Dehradun. You are from London?" He replied.

"Yes," I waited for him to say something more but getting no reply, I prompted, "So you teach criminal psychology, right?"

"Yes, I told you in the morning."

"I can make a guess by the title of what it entails, but I have never heard of this subject. What exactly is it?"

"It's a study of the criminals. Their minds, their intentions, actions and reactions," Mr Langhar replied.

"Oh," I said, perplexed by the description, "Is it bookish? Or do you provide field experience as well?" I asked, laughing.

"It's not CBI," He snapped at me. Geez! What a character. I just wanted to keep things light. But I guess he was one of those people who don't have a single funny bone in their body. I wanted to ask him more questions about his profession but decided against it. There would be more occasions in the future to prod and understand. It still baffled me how he was famous.

I saw Mr Nettles stop at my assigned table and say a few words to Mr and Mrs Vyas and then walk towards the bar to join rank with the Kumars.

Something about the way he stopped at the Vyases table was wrong, it was artificial. I can't pinpoint the reason why I knew that, but something about his stance when he was speaking with the Vyases made it look like it was just for show. His original target was to be with the Kumars, but he had stopped on the way to make it look like he was mingling with other guests.

The three of them- Mark Nettles, Shyam and Ira talked for a while at the bar- laughing loudly. But it was *off*! They were laughing, but their bodies were stiff and unnatural. And then all of a sudden Mr Nettles placed a hand on Shyam's shoulder, jerking his head towards the bartender. And then they walked out to the balcony together.

Why would they want to go towards the balcony for idle chatter? And why would the manager of the resort give two guests so much of his time? He had spared only seconds for the Vyases.

There was something about them that was rubbing me the wrong way, something suspicious. I didn't mind poking about.

Mr Langhar was engrossed listening to the band, and he didn't notice or didn't give the appearance of noticing as I slinked away to satisfy my curiosity.

10

The 'balcony' was, in essence, an open deck. It was big enough to fit 4 people at a time if they were comfortable squeezing uncomfortably together. There were no handrails, and the deck was perched right above the ocean.

The golden string lights gracing the front of the boathouse were missing from the sides, and the deck was masked in darkness. Feeble light escaping from indoors barely illuminated the faces of Mark Nettles, Ira Kumar and Shyam Kumar. Not that I could see them from my vantage point.

I covered my body as well as I could behind the glass door leading out to the balcony. Holding a beer in my hand, I nodded my head from time to time to portray that I was enjoying the music. But my ears were directed towards the conversation occurring out of my sight.

"Stop obsessing Shyam. It's too dangerous to change the plan. Not to add it will be impossible to work out the details. We will mess it up," Ira was saying, "Let's stick to the original plan. It has never failed us before."

"Everyone is here! They are enjoying the party. I think it will be safer," Shyam replied.

"Let's stick to the original plan, please. We don't need to change anything," Ira repeated.

"I agree with Ira. Don't leave too early," Mark Nettles said shortly.

I heard footsteps coming my way, and I moved just in time. The next second, the manager was back indoors. In my haste, I collided with the teenagers' table.

"Get your eyes tested," Jason threw at me in a mocking tone, much to the delight of Estelle Le Gall.

"Are you okay, Reece?" Mr Nettles halted at the noise. I was afraid he would ask me to explain my presence so close to the balcony, but his eyes were unsuspecting.

"Yes. It's quite dark here. I didn't see the table," I replied.

"It's mood lighting," Mr Nettles laughed out loud, "And are our young guests enjoying themselves?" Mr Nettles asked, smiling widely at the two teenagers as if they were little kids; not that the wide smile would have worked on little kids any better. Jason and Estelle glared at him.

"You all will love this!" Mr Nettles said unnerved and cleared his throat loudly before walking away.

At that instant, the lights were dimmed down further, and a spotlight set the centre of the stage ablaze. I found my way back to Mr Langhar's table in darkness. My watch showed 9.30pm on the dot.

"Ladies and Gentlemen, the time has come to reveal my surprise. Please welcome our star-performer T. Ted," Mr Nettles' voice boomed from the stage.

For a star-performer, the man who stepped onto the stage was a picture of anti-climax. He was more or less 5 feet tall. I couldn't say if that were because he was a teenager or just a short guy. His face was young and round though his build was skinny. His hair was cut short at the back but was long in front and arranged into spikey bangs over his forehead. He was dressed head to toe in black, but his feet were clad in golden sneakers, glittering in the spotlight.

"Thank you, Mr Nettles. My name is T. Ted," He said, looking down at that microphone. His voice was American.

"Have you heard of him?" Mr Langhar directed the question at me.

"Never saw, never heard," I whispered back.

"Let me take you on a journey that will be tattooed in your memory for the rest of your life," T. Ted strummed the electric guitar at full base to command silence from his pea-sized audience.

The local band members took their places back on stage except for their lead singer and the showstopper performance began.

T. Ted started slow. The black glossy Fender guitar was being prodded into the perfect setting. His guitar strap, a sharp contrasting blood-red colour was cutting into his shoulders at times and lying loose, almost escaping the contours of his left shoulder at other times, as he took the guitar in hand and tried to find the precise setting. The music was slow, laid back and the accessory band members looked a little perplexed. But just as I was about to turn my head to look at the expressions of my fellow audience, T. Ted's foot came down hard on a pedal, and deafening music filled the boathouse.

I didn't have to move my eyes from the stage to perceive the response of the audience. Their shouts mingled with mine were a sufficient indicator.

The deafening music, the repeated beating of the drums and amidst it all- at the centre, T. Ted's fingers were flying on the neck of the guitar. The player and the instrument were one.

T. Ted's hand was moving so fast. It was as if he was stroking the guitar instead of punctuating the strings. And not one beat was amiss.

His face was focused, his eyes closed. Only his body moved with the music- leaning to the right and then to the left, a little bent forward as he put his soul into the music.

I couldn't place the music in a specific genre. Sometimes it's better not to put things into the correct box. Just let it be for it can only be perfect outside the box. But the problem with leaving things outside the box is that it might turn into something that should not have existed.

My heartbeat rose along with the tempo, and my heart was jutting against my ribcage, trying to escape. It wanted to experience the bliss that was on T. Ted's face as he played. Why was I yearning for peace? Why was I feeling paranoid? Like I was on the brink of some horror.

I was unable to look away; wholly captivated by the way his hands were moving with lightning speed and the peace on his face. At last, there was an explosion of a sound, and I was free.

T. Ted hadn't spoken a single word; he had no need for them. His spiky bangs had melted and were plastering his forehead like spent oil wicks.

The performance ended at 10.00pm, and the star-performer received a standing ovation. I stood groggily on my feet, putting my hands together to applaud T. Ted's exit.

"He is going to be a star," Shyam said to us as we sat down.

"Wonder how much they paid him?" Norman Miller's voice said from behind us, "To come here in the middle of nowhere."

In the ensuing hum of discussions, a loud voice rang out.

"Mr Dale? Are you okay?"

11

Mr Dale's body was slumped forward. His shoulders were hunched in, chin touching his chest.

Om Vyas was standing over him, shaking his shoulder violently. My feet had a mind of their own, and I walked towards my employer robotically; the observing eyes of all, following my movement.

Mr Dale was visibly perspiring. His brow and forehead were covered in sweat, large beads accumulating and rolling down the bridge of his thin nose. The dark shirt was hiding the dampness, but as I touched his shoulder, the wetness doused my fingers. I repeated the question asked a moment ago by Mr Vyas- asking him whether he was okay?

He raised his head and brushed aside both Mr Vyas's and my hand and staggered up to his feet.

"Yes, I am bloody okay. Stop touching me," Mr Dale said in a slurred speech, "I shouldn't come to such communal events," He spat at us and reeled a few steps back. His eyes were bloodshot and unfocused. Mr Dale opened his mouth to lash out further, but no words came out. Opening the top two buttons of his shirt, his fingers trembling, Mr Dale staggered further back, hitting the teenagers' table much like I had earlier. Then in a daze, he turned and was out of sight in the blink of an eye.

I was debating whether to go after him when a voice said, "Somebody has taken advantage of the open bar."

"There's always one," Another voice added gleefully. Laughter rang out from the four corners and just like that the incident was forgotten.

"Come on, Reece. Don't do your duty today. Drunken people should be left alone," Evelyn Miller said, and taking my arm dragged me to the dance floor, "Let him enjoy his bliss."

Mr Nettles ordered the band to resume their occupation.

"Next dance is mine Reece," Noemie Le Gall proclaimed from her table. She was assessing Mrs Miller and me from her perch. Dressed in a white dress, wrapped tightly around her like a bandage, reminiscent of how mummies were wrapped up in ancient Egypt, her scarlet lips were stretched into an arrogant smile.

"Who does she think she is?" Evelyn whispered in my ears, giggling as we reached the open space in front of the stage.

"Who?" I feigned unworldliness.

"Noemie Le Gall! What's with that dress? How old is she- 16?" Mrs Miller replied, leading me in a circle, "She doesn't deserve her husband! Raphael is such a good man."

I kept quiet and nodded my head and allowed myself to be lead around the dance floor. I stopped enjoying my newfound popularity after five dances- two with Mrs Miller and three with Mrs Le Gall, taking turns.

The teenagers and the Kumars abandoned the party soon after Mr Dale had made his exit. Mark Nettles had not spoken to Ira and Shyam again, but his eyes had followed their departure. Whatever the trio was up to was happening tonight. I longed to find out more. But the two women incapacitated me. No amount of twitching and fidgeting had an effect. Eventually, I had to make an excuse of being thirsty to escape from the clutches of Noemie Le Gall.

"You don't dance Devin?" Mrs Vyas was saying as I removed my jacket and sank down in a chair.

"Not if I can help it," He smiled at her. Mr Langhar had joined the old Indian couple at my original table.

"I was saying that Devin would be surprised, but us old people have also heard of his fame," Mrs Vyas said to me.

"Oh, do tell," I said. My curiosity finally had a source to satiate it.

"The assistant police commissioner of Mumbai is a family friend. We know him for almost 20 years now," Mr Vyas said, "I think it was last month, yes last month, I remember because I bought this new diamond cufflinks and that was the first time I wore them. He and his wife were at our house for dinner, and he told us about Devin's genius and talent."

"The commissioner will be green with envy when I tell him we met *the* Devin Langhar in person," Mrs Vyas said.

"He is a kind man," Mr Langhar's said. His thin face was flushed.

"You said you were a criminology professor," I said taken aback.

"Oh, how humble! He helps the police solve complex and challenging cases. When the police have done everything they could think of, and there is no answer- Devin Langhar is the only hope," Mr Vyas said

"The assistant commissioner told us about this complicated case, in strictest confidence, of course. The police were exhausted. They didn't have any leads, no suspects, and after 6 months of running clueless, the department decided to enlist Devin's help. The assistant commissioner did add though about how many connections and strings he had to pull to bring Devin out to Mumbai. The police had no clue for 6 months, and then there was you – you solved it in a week," Mrs Vyas said, starry-eyed.

So that's why he was famous. He was a detective! I looked at Devin Langhar, astonished at this new revelation.

"Yes, I remember that case. It was in a small town near Mumbai. I cannot be more specific than that. It was one of those cases in which the murderer thinks that if he plants too many clues, haphazardly I should add, he could confuse the investigator and get away with it. It's good that criminals underestimate the ability of the law enforcement. That makes them so much easier to catch," Mr Langhar said, leaning back in his chair, a hint of restrained excitement in his eyes.

"But how did you catch the murderer?" I prompted him.

"I cannot go into specific details- it's confidential. In this particular case, the clues were all over the place and mind you there was no dearth of them. That always makes me suspicious. I would always take a crime with no clues than one with plenty of clues," Mr Langhar said, his eyes focused on the stage, "Once I eliminated the excess evidence and manufactured evidence- the criminal was right in front of me."

"You make it sound so simple," I quipped in. Surely this oversimplification of the revered profession was false and misleading.

"It's not simple," He replied in a crisp tone.

We all waited for him to add to his statement, but Mr Langhar was perfectly content with silence. It was unnatural. I have met many famous people in my old profession, aka a server. Those famous people couldn't stop talking, boasting and revealing all the things they had ever done. Here was a man who was perfectly content with not showcasing his abilities. Perfectly satisfied with not being the centre of attention by retelling his cases, which I was sure, he had solved heaps of by now.

I admired Mr Langhar's personality and admired the man himself. He was different.

I was about to ask a question to Mr Langhar, when Noemie stumbled towards our table, her feet unsteady in the clutches of high heels. She leaned on the table towards me, putting both her hands on the surface and knocking the discarded glass of Mr Dale on its side. The whiskey spilled out and stained the white tablecloth an amber brown.

"Reece let's dance," She said smiling, oblivious to her action.

"Thank you, Mrs Le Gall, but I am tired," I said.

"Tu es jeune!" She said scoffing, "Come."

Protesting more would have made me look discourteous, so I danced one last dance with her. Almost everyone had left the party by then- the Millers, Mrs Vyas and Raphael had left one by one.

The party finally came undone at 12.00am.

Om Vyas convinced Mr Langhar and me for a nightcap, and we retreated to Mr Langhar's villa for the remainder of the night.

12

I woke up the next morning later than usual. Instead of getting the blessing of a clear mind, I was groggy. My lower back ached where it had sunk between the sofa cushions. On my insistence, Om Vyas had taken the spare bedroom, and I was left to endure the tragedy of spending the night on a sofa that though looked like a million pounds was, in reality, all looks and no substance.

A splitting headache was giving company to the backache.

The Peridot colour curtains were drawn open, and the living room was bright. If nothing else, I would learn the names of rare colours before leaving this island. The layout was identical to the villa 'Jade', but the colour scheme was altered in harmony with the name of this villa.

Mr Langhar was sipping his coffee on the deck, bare feet propped up on the table.

"Help yourself to coffee or tea, whatever you prefer Reece," Mr Langhar said out loud as I got up to my feet. He didn't look up from the newspaper.

"How did you know it was me and not Mr Vyas?" I asked, "Does your detecting abilities stretch to routine life?"

"Because he left during the night. He was worried about leaving Mrs Vyas alone. There was a robbery in one of the villas just a night ago if you recall," He replied, chuckling. I seemed to be growing on him.

"I should be getting back. Hopefully, I still have a job," I laughed though it was the last thing I wanted to do. I should have returned to my villa last night. Mr Dale had been spectacularly intoxicated. What if he had required me during the night? Out loud, I said, "Thank you for accommodating me. Mr Dale would not have had any sympathy or tolerance."

"I will walk with you. I need breakfast," Mr Langhar said, throwing the newspaper aside.

I was astounded at the crumpled mess.

"Anything wrong?" Mr Langhar said, raising an eyebrow at my expression.

"I assumed, considering you are a detective, that you would be more organized. You know one who folds stuff with neat creases and perfect alignment," I replied, still very much taken aback at the condition of the newspaper.

"That's called stereotyping," He laughed out loud and walked ahead of me. He didn't correct me, though when I used the word 'detective'.

Even though Mr Langhar denied possessing order and method- his black Sunglasses were kept at the entry table along with the villa keycard and a white cap. He can disagree about being pernickety, but it was evident he had an orderly mind.

The sun was shining with a vengeance, and I was forced to use my palm to shield my face. The headache that was lurking in the background started its voyage to the forefront. For the first time, I longed for the dark, overcast days of London.

"You know what Mr Langhar, I will join you for breakfast. Let me just check up on Mr Dale- if that's okay?" I asked, amending my plans. My stomach wanted nourishment stat.

Mr Langhar nodded his affirmation, and I left him standing in the shade of the porch outside my villa.

The door to my room was ajar, but Mr Dale's bedroom door was shut. I knocked twice on his door but got no reply.

"Maybe he is in the bathroom," I said to Mr Langhar, trying the doorknob. The master bedroom was unlocked.

The first thing I felt was the cold. Goosebumps rose instantaneously on my exposed arms, and a shiver followed it. The air conditioning was blasting cold air at full capacity, it's fan clattering noisily. The jade green curtains were drawn so meticulously that even the most stubborn of light beam couldn't penetrate the thick curtains.

The only source of light was the door I had opened, and it threw a spotlight on the darkness.

My feet were like cement blocks. I forced myself to put one foot in front of the other. All the things that had scared me when I first stepped on this island, the known and the unknown was present in this room, right at this second. The horror and the discomfort I had experienced mixed with awe when I first looked at this paradise on earth seemed to be culminating into something tangible. And the horror element had taken a head lead.

Dizzy with apprehension, I walked towards Mr Dale and took a step back in shock.

Jeffrey Dale was lying on the left side of the king-size bed. His quilt was drawn all the way to his chin, and his mouth was partly open. His left-arm lay outside the warmth of the quilt, the wrist hanging freely from the edge of the bed.

His eyes were wide open, and the light grey colour had turned a shade lighter in the course of a night.

13

Panic replaced apprehension. My feet knotted together in my haste to leave the morbid room, and I fell headlong in the hallway.

Mr Langhar was standing in the same spot. His head jerked towards me as I crashed on the floor. He had a second of confusion on seeing me slumped on the ground. But the intelligent face read the terror on mine, and he marched inside the master bedroom, without exchanging a word.

My legs felt numb and heavy. I lay in a heap, knowing my legs wouldn't be able to bear my weight.

Mr Langhar came out after half a minute and picked up the cordless phone on the work desk. His face was straight and didn't betray his thoughts or emotions.

"This is Devin Langhar. Could you please send the resident doctor to the villa of Jeffrey Dale and the manager as well, immediately," He said in the phone, "What's the name of the villa?" He asked me.

"Jade," I whispered.

Mr Langhar repeated the name and put the phone back in its place.

"I didn't know they have a resident doctor," I said, clearing my throat and taking the help of the wall to stand up. Some part of me wanted to explain my overreaction and the lack of composure, but I padlocked that part and concentrated on keeping my voice steady.

"This is an island. It's essential they have a resident doctor," Mr Langhar said, watching me.

My legs gave a weak wobble under his intense scrutiny. In this moment I knew why he was revered. Mr Langhar's eyes were sharp, calculating, and I felt like he was reading my thoughts. I almost began to tell him how horrified I was at finding Mr Dale's dead body in this manner. The sound of activity outside the villa distracted me and spared me from further mortification.

Sooner than should be possible, Mr Nettles walked in.

"Is everything okay?" Mr Nettles asked. He was still wearing last night's clothes. The white coat was wrinkled badly on the sleeves, and the beige boat shoes were dirty and wet.

"It's Mr Dale. He is not breathing," I said, not wanting to say the word 'dead' out loud.

Before the manager could respond, we heard a buggy pull up outside and come to an abrupt stop.

"What's wrong?" A man hurried in.

Mr Langhar pointed at Mr Dale's bedroom and followed the doctor and the manager inside.

I stood right next to the entrance, close enough to see what was happening but not allowing myself to get any closer. Mr Langhar was standing at the doctor's shoulder, watching him examine the long-lost patient.

"Well, he is no more with us," The doctor finally straightened and pushed his thin-rimmed spectacles back in its place. He must be in his early 20s. He was wearing a plain yellow t-shirt, but he had a stethoscope around his neck to profess his identity.

"Heart-attack?" Mr Nettles asked, nodding his head. He was standing in front of the dresser kept opposite the bed.

"The cause of death cannot be established until a post-mortem examination is done. You should notify the police, Mr Nettles," The doctor said.

"Post-mortem! Police! Dr Samir, he is an ancient man, was! He is what, in his late 60s?" Mr Nettles looked towards me to confirm his estimate.

"68 I think," I said.

"See. This is a natural death. I know you haven't had much experience, but a heart attack is the number one killer at that age," Mr Nettles said, "You cannot bring police to our resort. Imagine if the word spreads! Our business is fragile and built on reputation," Mr Nettles added severely.

The doctor looked at Mr Langhar reflexively. His mind had picked up that Mr Langhar was the man with the highest authority.

"Dr Samir is right. This is a case of sudden death, and it's his duty as well as yours Mr Nettles, to notify the police," He said in a smooth voice, stopping the protests of the manager, "Would you stay with the body, doctor? I will accompany Mr Nettles to the main office."

"But police on resort property. Like death wasn't enough," The manager said hysterically and allowed himself to be guided outside by the Indian detective.

14

If you had asked me this question six months back- do I see myself holidaying in Maldives six months from now? You would have heard a reluctant but an unequivocal no. I hadn't even heard of this Island nation six months ago; forget about planning a vacation or having enough money to do that. And yet here I was six months later, at the most beautiful place on earth, having a perpetual blue-sky holiday, living and breathing the *greatest nightmare* of my 24 years of life.

The problem I had envisioned two days prior- of me quitting this daily degradation that I called a job and getting a lousy recommendation was a much better alternative than my present position.

Now I was going to be unemployed for the rest of my life. Who was going to hire an assistant, under whose care his employer died? *I was doomed.*

Sitting in the living room, looking at the endless ocean, it didn't calm me as poets, and literary geniuses claim- that the vastness of the sea always put your problems in perspective. It didn't assuage any of my fears, any of my hellish thoughts and I sat numb and still, till the main door swung open.

Mr Langhar walked inside, accompanied by two men. They were wearing plain white shirts, but I knew they were the police. Mr Nettles was trailing behind, looking worse than I was feeling.

"I am surprised to see you here, Devin. But nonetheless a splendid surprise," The older man was saying as he followed Mr Langhar in.

Mr Langhar introduced the older man as Inspector Rashid, and the younger chap was junior Inspector Hamid.

"I want a statement from you Reece after I have examined the crime scene," Inspector Rashid said to me.

"Crime scene?" Mr Nettles whined. My thoughts mirrored his words- the crime scene? *Could this get any worse?*

The forensic team, the inspectors had brought with them from Malé, was directed inside. I resumed my place near the doorway, being able to see what was happening without stepping inside.

A policeman was dusting for fingerprints on the bedside table, and a photographer was taking photos from multiple viewpoints.

"Doctor, what can you tell me," Inspector Rashid asked the police examiner who had taken over the dead body.

Dr Samir was standing over his shoulder, educating and training himself for the future event of finding himself in the vicinity of another death.

"He died somewhere between 2.30am, and 3.30am last night," The doctor said without looking up.

"Cause of death?" Inspector Rashid asked.

"There are no external injuries. I cannot say for certain until I have completed the post mortem examination."

"Is there a possibility of this being a natural death?" Inspector Hamid asked.

"There is a possibility that lizards are the progeny of dinosaurs and it's a matter of time that they grow up to gigantic proportion and kill us all one day. You will have to wait till I have done a full examination," The doctor repeated a little impatiently, "Till then treat this as a crime scene." He stood up and removed the latex gloves.

"Did he have any medical conditions?" Inspector Rashid asked me, trying to smoothen his smile.

"He was a diabetic. He was taking Insulin injections for that," I replied.

"High blood pressure?" The doctor asked.

"I don't think so. Mr Dale never mentioned it," I said.

After a moment of reflection, Inspector Rashid led the way out to the living room.

Mr Nettles was the first one to speak, "Inspector, I know how seriously you take your job, but he was an old man! All this investigation is unnecessary."

"Mr Nettles, you are the manager. I am sure you have a thousand things to do. Don't let us keep you," Inspector Rashid said, dismissing Mr Nettles. He didn't speak another word till the manager had left the villa.

"Now Reece, you discovered the body?" Inspector Rashid settled himself down on the sofa. He was a well-built man, and his shirtsleeves tightened around his arms as he sat down.

"Yes, I came to check if Mr Dale was awake, and I found him cold," I replied, taking a deep breath.

"You didn't hear anything during the night?" Inspector Rashid asked.

I was terrified by his tone and the way the Inspectors were eyeing me, but then I remembered that I had the perfect alibi. *I was in Mr Langhar's villa*! That gave me a lot of reassurance as I narrated the 'why' I didn't hear anything during the night to Inspector Rashid's satisfaction.

"When did you last see him alive?" Inspector Hamid asked, his pen flying over the pages of his notepad.

"At the party. We were all there- I mean the guests staying in the neighbouring villas. Mr Dale left before me, and that was the last time I saw him."

"Did anything stand out?" Inspector Rashid asked.

"What do you mean?" I asked warily. A lot of things had stood out in the past 3 days. But I didn't want to get involved with the police.

"Last night. Why did Jeffrey Dale leave the party early?" Inspector Rashid asked.

"He wasn't feeling well. But we all assumed it was because he drank too much alcohol."

"Assumed?" Inspector Rashid lingered on the word.

I didn't reply to that.

"You didn't come back to your villa after the party?" Inspector Rashid asked in the same suspicious tone.

"No, like I said, we had a nightcap at Mr Langhar's villa. You can ask him," I said, a little smug.

Mr Langhar was sitting next to Inspector Rashid, not looking at us and staring at the ceiling. *He wasn't even listening.*

"Mr Langhar told us that there was a robbery in the villa across from this a couple of days back. Could this be a robbery gone bad?" Inspector Hamid said, his voice quivering as he said the name of the celebrated detective.

"Is anything missing from the villa?" Inspector Rashid asked me.

"I can't be sure. I wasn't that familiar with Mr Dale's possessions. I don't know if he had anything valuable with him," I replied.

"You were his personal assistant," Inspector Rashid said flatly.

"Yes."

"How long have you worked for him?" Inspector Rashid asked.

"Six months."

"And you do not know if he bought anything valuable with him?" Inspector Rashid asked patronizingly.

"No, do you really expect me to know that?" I exclaimed loudly, my breath starting to hitch up. I knew it! They were going to blame it on me!

"What can you tell me about your boss?" Inspector Rashid asked, ignoring my protest.

"Not much. Like I said, I took this job six months ago."

"What was his profession?" Inspector Hamid asked. That question attracted Mr Langhar's attention, and he fixed his brown eyes on me.

"He had a newspaper in America, some 15 years ago-till it shut down that is. He was living in London for a year now," I replied but seeing the unsatisfied expression on the senior and junior inspectors faces I added, "He was an exceedingly secretive man. I did lowly jobs for him like getting his coffee or getting his laundry done. He didn't confide in me. But he always carried this black pocketbook with him. Maybe that could help you. He used to write in that all the time," I said. Hopefully, this will distract them, and they will stop persecuting me.

"Hamid look for this diary. What did he write in this diary?" Inspector Rashid asked.

"I am telling you I don't know. We were not best mates. I never saw what he was writing in it," I replied patiently.

"You never got curious?" Inspector Rashid said.

"No Inspector, I don't have a habit of reading other people's private diary!" I replied coldly.

"Sir, you have to see this," Inspector Hamid's shocked voice exploded from inside the bedroom.

I followed Mr Langhar and the senior inspector to the dressing room. It was a small room between the bedroom and bathroom. Mr Dale's suitcases lay open to the public eye on the marble bench inside. Inspector Hamid had removed the top layer of his clothes, and they lay discarded on the bench.

"Look at this," Inspector Hamid said and moved aside.

The bottom of the suitcase was fitted with deep padded cutouts. There was a binocular, two tape recorders and an empty space that looked like it was meant for a camera but the camera was missing.

"There's no sign of the diary Sir," Inspector Hamid added quietly looking directly at Mr Langhar.

15

"They are very powerful," Inspector Rashid said looking through the binoculars

"No tapes in the tape recorder," Mr Langhar added.

"What was in the diary? You told us Mr Dale owned a newspaper. Why would a newspaper owner require binoculars or tape recorders?" Inspector Rashid pounced on me.

"My answer is not going to change. I don't know," I said.

"Find the diary Hamid," Inspector Rashid barked at his junior.

The villa was searched top to bottom, but the diary was nowhere to be found.

"It's not here, Sir," Inspector Hamid appealed with tired eyes, dropping the dirty clothes back in the laundry basket.

"This is officially a crime scene now," Inspector Rashid said directing his forensic team to lock it down.

"Who else knew about the diary, besides you Reece?" Mr Langhar asked.

"Mr Dale was always scribbling in it, all places and at all times. Anyone could have seen him," I replied.

"Your answers are very convenient," Inspector Rashid glared at me, "For your neck."

"It's the truth that is convenient," I said in a flat tone. The police were not going to get a rise out of me.

"You can't stay in this villa," Inspector Rashid said, directing a policeman to stand guard.

"Where am I supposed to sleep?" I asked dejected and hungry. It was late afternoon. My head was splitting open, and my stomach was hurting from hunger.

"You can take the spare bedroom in my villa," Mr Langhar replied and left with the two inspectors before I could thank him.

It didn't take me long to pack up my stuff. All I had was a suitcase and a handbag. Both were zipped and ready in a quarter of an hour.

I was starving at this point. The clock showed 4.00pm, and I prayed to be lucky enough to find some sustenance at the restaurant. Whatever little luck I had left.

The policeman was sitting in the living room and watching television. He didn't look away from the TV as I opened the front door and left.

Outside I was expecting everything to be quiet, and hence I jumped up with surprise to find Estelle Le Gall coming up the steps.

"I am really sorry about what happened," She said quickly, one word toppling over another. Her eyes were wide open, and the natural expression of arrogance and disdain was missing from her face. It felt as if she had rehearsed the opening statement many times and yet when the time had come to deliver it, had utterly failed to tap into the rehearsal. She knew it, and I knew it and, I was curious to understand why a teenager would be interested in offering her sympathies?

"That's kind of you," I replied.

"Why was the police here? How did he die?" She asked in an off-hand tone, but her fingers were pulling the end of the white scarf around her neck.

"Well it could be a heart attack, or it could be anything in the world. The doctor, the one who examines the dead body, is going to check things. Are you okay?" I asked.

"Oui je vas bien. I mean I am fine. He wasn't feeling well yesterday, and he is an old man. Was," She said more to herself than to me and walked away.

I didn't fully comprehend this interaction. Did Estelle have something to do with this murder or did she know something? I shuddered at the word 'murder', but there was no other reason why she would be interested in this death. No, Estelle must know something or this 180-degree change in personality couldn't be explained. And why was she standing outside the crime scene? She could have offered her condolences to me anywhere but to be standing right outside in the heat and waiting for me to make an appearance was weird.

She must be waiting outside to overhear the conversations of the police! And then would have chosen me as a soft-target to get the rest of the information. She knew the police and Mr Langhar would see through her, but she could take her chances with me. Here was a teenage girl with a lot of cunning!

I was mulling over the strange encounter, as I dropped my bags on the porch of Mr Langhar's villa and then walked on to the restaurant for my first meal of the day. And there I was surprised for the third time today.

The arrangement of the tables was exactly like the next day of the robbery, or yesterday to be exact, though it seemed yesterday was weeks ago.

Ira Kumar was the first one to ambush me-

"Oh, Reece, I am sorry about what happened. I can't imagine what you must be going through! We saw Mr Dale last night, and then something like this happening out of nowhere!" She had her claws tightly around my right arm, and I was more scared of her talons than the police.

Ira began dragging me to the head of the table. Evelyn Miller had graced that chair yesterday, and today I was being shoved into it.

"Moments like these are a reminder to live our life to the fullest each and every day," Mr Vyas said pensively.

"Was it a heart attack?" Mrs Vyas asked.

"The doctor is not sure about the cause of death," I said cautiously.

Norman and Evelyn Miller exchanged a glance between themselves at that statement.

"Let me say how sorry we are," Evelyn said.

"Thank you, but I feel like an imposter accepting condolences. I didn't know him that well. I was his personal assistant," Hopefully, this will stop people from offering me their sympathies.

"This island is cursed, first the robbery in our villa and now the death of a poor man. I am regretting the day we decided to come here for a vacation," Mr Miller all but spat out the last word.

"Norman, please don't imagine things! Nothing is cursed," Mrs Miller said.

"Are they going to do an autopsy?" Shyam asked me.

"I guess so," I replied. I didn't know how much I was allowed to disclose.

"Autopsy?" Noemie asked over her cup of coffee. Raphael explained the term to her in rapid French.

"Oh, that's dreadful!" Noemie exclaimed in English. She closed her eyes in disgust and took a sip.

Estelle entered the restaurant at that instant. She walked swiftly to stand behind her mother's chair, extending a protective palm on her mother's shoulder. But the stream of people entering the restaurant was not complete and Jason Miller walked in next. He swayed on the entrance, unsure of his place in the room and then took long strides to a vacant chair at the shared table.

"I agree with you, Noemie. Why subject a poor old man to something so dreadful. We all know it will be something related to old age. The doctors should really have common sense," Evelyn said.

"He was sick last night," Ira added.

"Yes, Ira dear. You remember Om, how he fainted towards the end of the party?" Mrs Vyas said.

"He took a drink too many last night," Om Vyas replied, giving a nudge in the ribs of Norman Miller.

"It was the beginning of the end for him," Noemie said mildly.

"Devin, there you are- you can tell us more!" Om Vyas shouted at the new entry.

"Excuse me?" Mr Langhar was caught off guard coming into the restaurant and took a step back at the loud noise.

"Jeffrey Dale's sudden death! I am sure you are in the middle of it, considering your reputation," Om Vyas said, "In fact, I should say that the police are lucky that Devin is here to assist them," He added for the benefit of all the guests.

"Are you the police?" Norman Miller asked.

"No."

"He is humble. Typical! He has helped Indian police countless times and even International Police on occasions," Om Vyas gave the gossip to everyone.

"A real-life Sherlock Holmes?" Raphael said grinning.

"Why does the police need assistance? Are the police considering Mr Dale's death suspicious?" Shyam asked. This was the second time he had asked that question.

Not to say his wife was friendlier today. Yesterday Ira wouldn't spare a glance at me. Today she was the first one to show her sympathy.

And then there was the third member of the trio- Mark Nettles. He was persistent in his insistence on treating the demise of Jeffrey Dale as a natural death. He might have gotten away with it as well if not for the presence of Mr Langhar.

"This is a police matter. That makes it confidential by default," Mr Langhar said, his face showing impatience.

"So you are helping the police. I knew it," Om Vyas said, "He is brilliant."

At once, Mr Miller's back stiffened, and he sat up straighter. Shyam turned his head away, becoming interested in the view of the ocean.

Devin Langhar's eyes scanned the faces of 11 people sitting around. He sighed and then went on to sit at a corner table, effectively implying that he was not going to be a part of their conversation.

16

Though it hadn't been said out loud, the word 'Murder' hung around me like a putrid stench, making me wish I had never stepped on this island. Was this place any different from a dirty back alley where hideous crimes transpire, and innocent people become victims indirectly or directly?

I was folding the blanket, still in a haze, when Mr Langhar walked in.

"Inspector Rashid called, he will be here soon with the post-mortem report. I have ordered some breakfast. You are welcome to it," He said and retreated.

Devin Langhar was undeniably a hard man to understand. His demeanour was that of an extremely private person; walking and singing to his own tune; a man who would not be bothered by the ways of the world. But on the flip side, Mr Langhar had oodles of tact, and all his actions were saturated with kindness and consideration. Both aspects of his personality were poles apart, and he was a living, breathing enigma.

"Thank you again, Mr Langhar for letting me stay here," I said, sitting down across from him at the deck table.

The breakfast tray was filled with golden-brown toast cut in triangles, and hard-boiled eggs, goat cheese and mushroom omelette and a stack of fluffy pancakes with strawberries piling up on top. A white bowl had an array of individual pods of jams and whipped butter. A miniature ceramic jug was filled to the brim with maple syrup. It was a feast, whenever I had a meal at Embassy resort, and the recent developments had not influenced their standard.

The doorbell rang in synchrony with Mr Langhar taking the last bite of his toast. I obliged him by getting the door; it was a reflex for me anyways.

Inspector Rashid was standing outside with Inspector Hamid in tow. They were wearing starched white shirts today as well. The senior Inspector's face showed annoyance on finding me at the door. Nevertheless, he said in a composed tone-

"Morning Reece."

I responded in kind and led them to the living room.

"This is a nice villa," Inspector Hamid said, sitting on the sofa. But a hard look from his senior shut him up from further comment, and Mr Langhar jumped to the point an instant later-

"What's the verdict?"

"The preliminary time of death still stands. Jeffrey Dale died between 2.30am, and 3.30am," Inspector Hamid opened the brown file.

"That's as specific as the doctor is comfortable in getting," Inspector Rashid added, "Go on."

"Cause of death- uncertain," Inspector Hamid read, "A large quantity of phenobarbitone was found in his blood. But the doctor cannot say if that amount was sufficient to cause death. He did add that we have to factor in the old age, but he is still not comfortable assigning blame to the drug. Substantial quantity of alcohol was also found in the body of the deceased."

"So it was not a heart attack or any natural cause as the killer wanted us to believe," Mr Langhar said more to himself than the room.

"We didn't find any fingerprint except that of Jeffrey Dale and Reece's," Inspector Rashid said blatantly staring at me, "And we can rule out robbery. Nothing is missing from the villa beside the 'black diary' and the camera. His debit and credit cards, cash, his watch, mobile phone everything was there. Hamid tell him about the other thing."

"Now the odd discovery Sir. A needle mark was found on the deceased's inner arm on the left side. The doctor says phenobarbitone was taken or given orally and he is certain that it was not injected," Inspector Hamid said.

"Reece, you said that he didn't take any drugs besides the Insulin. What about the phenobarbitone?" Inspector Rashid asked.

"No, he didn't take any. Was this phenobarbitone given to him during the party?" I asked.

"Yes. We need to go over everything Jeffrey Dale ate and drank that night," Inspector Rashid said.

"I got him his first drink. He had bourbon. After that, I can't help you. I wasn't sitting with him," I said.

"We have to get his glass tested to confirm the presence of the drugs. I have spoken to the manager, and he will take us to the boathouse later. I instructed them to lock it down after we discovered the body yesterday," Inspector Hamid said, smug at his foresight.

"That's not going to help you," I said.

"Did they clear away the things?" Inspector Hamid asked, upset, "I specifically told them not to touch anything."

"No. Mr Dale's glass was knocked over at the party. You can't test it," I replied.

"What? Who knocked it over?" Inspector Rashid asked forcefully, sitting straighter.

"I am sure it was an accident," I replied.

I didn't want to implicate anyone but what were the chances of Noemie Le Gall knocking over that particular glass among all the drinks that were on the table? If she poisoned the glass, she would want to remove the evidence. And then there was her daughter. The way Estelle was behaving, especially around her mother after the death of Mr Dale, shielding her in a way, it was strange. Those two were not innocent but were they guilty of murder?

"Who Reece? This is important," Inspector Rashid asked.

"It was Noemie Le Gall," I replied resigned, "I don't think it was intentional..."

"Jeffrey Dale was taking Insulin for his diabetes," Mr Langhar said abruptly, "Insulin is taken subcutaneously," He added, pacing now.

"What are you talking about Devin?" Inspector Rashid said after a minute of watching Mr Langhar pace from one end to the other.

"I need to go back to the villa," He replied impatiently.

17

We found the duty inspector sprawled across the couch in the living room. He scurried up to his feet as the door burst open with a bang, and we witnessed him smoothening his hair and turning off the TV at the same time.

Inspector Rashid eyed him viciously and dismissed him.

Mr Langhar ignoring all rushed to the mini-fridge kept in the entryway.

"Reece, what do you make of this?" Mr Langhar was holding the fridge's door open and was pointing at the middle rack.

"It's the insulin box," I replied, confused at Mr Langhar's excitement.

He sighed impatiently at my dimness before talking-

"Would Jeffrey Dale open a new box if the old box had a vial left?" He asked, showing me both the boxes.

"No, he would have finished that one first," I said. Somewhere in the back of my head, a tiny bell was jingling, but my consciousness was two steps behind.

And Devin Langhar was five steps ahead.

"We have four vials missing from the new box," Mr Langhar said showing us the box, "And the top box has one vial left."

"What has that got to do with his murder?" Inspector Rashid asked, as incapable of making the connection as I was.

"Insulin can be used as a poison. In fact, it is an extremely competent murder weapon," Mr Langhar said in a careful monotone.

"But he died because of phenobarbitone," Inspector Hamid said.

"I think he died because Insulin was used as a poison. That's why his left arm has the needle mark. The killer must have injected Insulin directly into his blood," Mr Langhar explained.

"Two murder weapons? That's unlikely Devin. Maybe Jeffrey Dale forgot about the top box? You can't say with full confidence that he didn't use the 4 vials in the lower box," Inspector Rashid said.

"Of course, but knowing human nature, understanding how certain personalities work, I can be confident in saying that Jeffrey Dale would have finished this box first. He was a systematic person. Did you see the cutouts in his suitcase? They were handmade and fit like a glove around his devices," Mr Langhar said.

"He's right Inspector. Mr Dale was crazy about order and method, especially about his personal belongings." I said.

"Do you mean to say that two people decided to kill Jeffrey Dale on the same night?" Inspector Rashid stared at Mr Langhar.

"Or the same killer used two methods," Mr Langhar replied quietly.

"Is there a way to trace Insulin in the blood?" Inspector Rashid asked after a moment's deliberation.

"I will ask the doctor." Inspector Hamid said, scribbling in his notepad.

"How did the killer get inside the villa?" Inspector Rashid inquired.

"The back door was unlocked, or I should say it was broken into. There are scuff marks around the lock," Mr Langhar replied.

"Why didn't you mention this yesterday?" Inspector Rashid said rudely.

"Because I didn't know if it was murder yesterday. Those scuff marks could be there from before," Mr Langhar answered in the same Zen tone.

"Who is staying next to your villa?" Inspector Rashid asked me.

"On the left are Mr and Mrs Vyas and on the right the Millers. But..." I began.

"The Millers! The robbery occurred in their villa. The doctor said the brand name of the medicine stolen from them matched the chemical formula found in the victim's body- phenobarbitone," Inspector Rashid said, putting air quotation marks around the word robbery, "If it walks like a duck and quacks like a duck- then it's a duck."

"Listen I found the main door unlocked as well yesterday morning," I said hastily before Inspector Rashid could interrupt me again.

Absolute silence met my information.

"So the killer could have simply walked in," Inspector Hamid said.

"The main door could be opened from inside to mislead the police," Mr Langhar said.

"It's irrelevant. Even if Insulin can be used as a poison, we cannot ignore the phenobarbitone found in the victim's body, which was *unquestionably* used," Inspector Rashid said, "First things first. Hamid take the insulin boxes to the forensic lab. However, I doubt we will find anything, no offence Devin. Then find the manager and ask him to tell the guests that we need to talk to all of them. This is a murder investigation," Inspector Rashid dispatched his junior and then turned to face me, "Reece, please excuse us for a minute?"

I got up without saying another word and walked into my old bedroom. I slammed the door behind me, but my hand was firmly on the knob to prevent it from clicking into place. After waiting for a few seconds, I pulled the door slightly towards myself, creating a gap and providing me access to sound from the living room on the other side.

18

"Devin, I hope we have come to the same conclusion. The murderer is someone from one of the villas," Inspector Rashid began almost immediately.

"Yes, that's evident. I took the liberty to talk to the guard, and he is certain that no one from the main island entered this restricted area," Mr Langhar said," The procession of waiters stopped at 11.30am. Moreover, the waiters never ventured into the vicinity of the private villas. They walked on the beach to reach the boathouse."

"That's all very well. What I am trying to say is that the list contains the name of Reece Oberoi," Getting no response from Mr Langhar he added, "And you are trusting him with private and confidential case details."

"He didn't kill Jeffrey Dale. Reece was in my villa, asleep on the couch, on the night in question," Mr Langhar said dismissively.

"Yes. But the phenobarbitone was not given at night; it was given during the party. Reece had plenty of chances to poison his employer's glass. He got him his first drink, and he is the only one with any connection to the victim. He should be treated like everyone- a potential suspect," Inspector Rashid elaborated the case against me.

Despite the fact that Inspector Rashid was building a case against me, I could see his point. Soon the police will discover how Jeffrey Dale treated me like a servant, and that will complete the police's case- they will have a motive.

But I was not the only one who knew Mr Dale on this island. I was not the only one with a hatred for Jeffrey Dale. My mind raced back to the night of the blackmail when the first crack had appeared in the mirror, reflecting this paradise, and I breathed calmly. All was not lost yet.

"You attended the lecture I presented in Colombo two years ago?" Mr Langhar asked.

"Yes, it was invaluable. Your research and theories have helped in countless cases, my friend," Inspector Rashid's voice was soft with admiration.

"I have attempted to merge the branches of human psychology with criminal psychology. I am not talking about deviancy here. We have enough people in the Police force who do that. The systems, the protocols and the factors that help to catch serial killers or killers with serious mental derangement are in place for a few decades now. I specialize in solving crimes where no deviancy is apparent. And in those crimes, human psychology is instrumental. I help the police see how the criminal thinks, acts and reacts. I help them understand the mind of a criminal."

"Devin, I didn't mean to doubt your expertise," Inspector Rashid replied quickly.

"Reece is a young man whose life has not been easy. He has survived on the charity of other people. But he is not vindictive about it- jealous yes, vindictive no. Jeffrey Dale was his employer, his daily bread, and it's against Reece's disposition or any other man or women like him to destroy their daily bread. Their instinct goes against killing their paycheck. No amount of humiliation would ever affect him to take such a drastic action. He is simply not the type," Mr Langhar finished with a final note in his voice.

My ears were red and hot, but I have always known that much about me. All my life has been about self-preservation and getting what I want in the only way I know- being friends with rich boys and then men in my later years. They were unnecessarily cruel and ragged me till my smile was a ghost on my lips, but I couldn't abandon their friendship if I can call it that. They were my ride, my food, my first beer, and my designer jacket. It was a symbiotic relationship. They ragged on me to make themselves feel better. And I, in turn, used them as much as they used me. It shouldn't be embarrassing to hear the reality out loud, and I wasn't embarrassed. I do what I do to survive, and I was grateful that Mr Langhar appreciated that instead of judging me and holding it against me.

I heard Mr Langhar call my name from the other side, and I sucked in a deep breath before approaching the two.

"We were discussing that it shouldn't get out that *I think* Insulin was used as a murder weapon. I want the murderer to think that he or she has been cunning and gotten away with it," Mr Langhar said.

"That makes sense," I replied shortly. Mr Langhar looked curiously at me, but as was characteristic of him, he didn't bother asking questions to satisfy his curiosity. He didn't need to ask questions to get the answers. Devin Langhar could read a man like an open book, like he had read me. I should have been wary of him, but I was amazed by his gift and felt cavernous respect for his compassion.

"Let me double-check if the pool door is locked," Inspector Rashid said and went to the master bathroom that provided access to the pool.

"Devin," Inspector Rashid called out from inside. We found him squatting near the bathtub, and he was holding something in his hand, "How did we miss this?"

"What is it?" I asked edging closer.

"It's a tiepin," Mr Langhar replied, holding it and peering carefully at it.

It was a thin golden pin with a sapphire at the end. Mr Langhar flipped it and the initials JB were engraved on the back.

"It is not Mr Dale's," I said, shocked at finding a real clue.

"It wasn't here yesterday," Mr Langhar said.

"How can you be sure? We miss clues all the time. That's why we seal the crime scene so we can come back and look at it," Inspector Rashid said, grabbing a tissue paper and carefully wrapping the tiepin in it.

"Did the killer drop it here accidentally?" I asked.

"It proves your theory that the killer was in the villa," Inspector Rashid said to Mr Langhar.

"The tiepin wasn't here yesterday," Mr Langhar repeated.

19

"Whom should we start with?" Inspector Rashid said, "I am not jumping to any conclusion. We are going to talk to everyone present at the party. But if you count my experience- we could save a lot of time if I go and arrest Norman Miller right now."

"You can't arrest him without a motive," Mr Langhar said shortly, "Let's begin with the eyes and ears of the resort."

Mark Nettles' office was situated on the main island. The over-water villas boardwalk ended in a sand-covered path leading into the main island that held the manager's office and the reception area.

The sandy path was flanked with tall palm trees, and only a narrow alley of clear blue sky was visible above. Orchids of vivid colours, rising from makeshift vases made out of coconut shells were tied to the tree trunks.

Mr Nettles' office building was twice the size of the housekeeping hut. A woman was sitting behind the desk, dressed the same as Hassan in loose cotton white shirt and Maroon pants.

She rose to greet us, "How can I help you?"

"The manager please," Inspector Rashid said briefly, flashing his identification.

The poor woman leapt in surprise. Her pen went flying from her hand and clacked loudly as the plastic made contact with the tiled floor. It then rolled off under the filing cabinet where I knew it was going to die, forgotten. She picked up the phone speedily and dialled. It was comical that we could hear the phone ringing inside, making this display of importance redundant.

"Sir, the police are here to see you... He will be right with you," She said the latter part of the sentence for our benefit.

The door to the manager's office was thin, and we could clearly hear the sounds that were coming from inside, at least I could. It sounded like someone that is to say Mark Nettles was moving with the speed of a tornado. A drawer was pulled and then shut again with force, and then another drawer was pulled and slammed back into its place. The next sound of tape being pulled off. By the loud protesting noise it made- I was sure it was duct tape. The sound of tape pulling was repeated a few times, and then the door opened immediately after that.

"Sorry for the delay. I was on an important call," Mr Nettles said, dabbing his forehead, "How can I help?"

"Let's go inside your office," Inspector Rashid said.

"Yes, please come in. It's a little messy," Mr Nettles replied, closing the door behind us. The pompousness he had radiated in our early encounters was absent. Today Mr Nettles was a nervous ball of wool that has been played to the point of abuse by a cat with cutting claws.

The manager's office was a closed shoebox. I was expecting something flashy, as per his personality and the bleakness was disconcerting. The office had an iron desk in the centre of the room, and it was littered with a thousand papers. The chair behind it was the same as that of the receptionist, bare and uncomfortable.

A framed picture of Embassy resort was serving as the sole piece of décor. In front of the opposite wall were two medium-size cardboard boxes. The mouths of the boxes were sealed off with brown duct tape, and a single roll of duct tape was sitting on top.

And Mr Langhar's eyes were fixed on the boxes.

"Inspector you have to clear this matter up immediately. Our guests are getting disturbed. I fear our business is going to get severely affected by this... business," Mr Nettles fumed.

"This is a serious crime, Mr Nettles. It's a murder investigation now," Inspector Rashid said sternly.

"Murder?" Mr Nettles said with a quiver in his voice, "But why? How?"

"Jeffrey Dale was poisoned. When was the last time you saw Mr Dale alive?" Inspector Rashid asked.

"He said he wasn't feeling well and left the party at 10.00. He had too much to drink. We always have one guest who gets carried away when there's an open bar," He rolled his eyes and continued, "I escorted him out and even offered to drive him myself to Jade but he refused."

"Drive him to what?" Inspector Rashid asked, confused.

"It's the name of his villa."

"That was the last time you saw him?" Mr Langhar asked.

"No. Later during the night, I was out on the balcony of the boathouse having a drink. Now I can't be sure because it was dark, but I saw Mr Dale walking on the beach."

"What time was this?" Inspector Rashid asked.

"11.00. I know it exactly because I was surprised. I thought Mr Dale had gone back to his villa."

"Was he alone?" Mr Langhar asked.

"No, he was walking with a woman. I couldn't tell who it was from so far out. It was pitch-black. I could just make out the silhouette of a woman," He replied.

Mr Langhar and Inspector Rashid exchanged a look at that revelation. The Inspector's theory of Norman Miller being the killer was falling apart. A woman was with Mr Dale before he died.

"The couple from Dubai, Shyam and Ira, have they been here to your resort before?" Mr Langhar asked.

The Inspector and I looked at Mr Langhar, wearing similar expressions of puzzlement.

"Yes, they have been here twice before. Our service is excellent- quite a few of our guests return to stay with us," The manager replied in an off-hand manner.

Mr Nettles made it sound like he barely knew the Dubai couple. But I knew they were well acquainted with one another. *And they were up to something last night.* I wanted to ask about that, but I knew Inspector Rashid was looking for a way to kick me out of this investigation. I can tell Mr Langhar about my observations later.

"Did you see anything unusual at the party?" Inspector Rashid asked.

"I am sorry I can't help you, I was making sure our guests are having a pleasant time."

20

"Please, Inspector get this misunderstanding cleared up. It was a natural death or an accident. Who would want to kill an old man?" Mr Nettles opened the door for us.

"What's in these boxes?" Mr Langhar asked, pointing at the cardboard cases.

"It's our toiletries supply. It got delivered last night. I am yet to put it away in the storage room," Mr Nettles replied, his face expressionless.

"Shyam told us that they are the supplier?" Mr Langhar asked.

"Yes. Why are you asking about this?" Mr Nettles inquired.

"You must know the Kumars well?" Mr Langhar asked another question.

"It's his company. I deal with factory people," Mr Nettles replied, opening his office door a little wider.

I was the first one to step out, and I collided with Shyam. He was standing directly outside Mr Nettles office's door.

"What are you doing here?" He asked me in a loud voice.

"And you are?" Inspector Rashid asked, flashing his convenient identification.

"Shyam Kumar and this is my wife Ira," He replied after a pause, "What's going on? Is this about the death of that old man?"

"Yes," Inspector Rashid said after getting a nod from Mr Langhar, "It's a murder investigation. He was poisoned."

"This is terrible. After I have paid so much money the least this resort can do is provide good security for us," Shyam said.

"I doubt the resort can provide security for crimes committed from within," I said.

"From within Reece? It must be one of the band members. These musicians take drugs and alcohol. They have homicidal tendencies. You should look at them, Inspector," Shyam replied.

Ira nodded her head vehemently, treating the words of her husband as the words of Gita.

"Do you think we all got poisoned? Did you test the food and drinks?" Shyam asked, horror written on his face, as this possibility occurred to him. Either he was an excellent actor, or he genuinely didn't have anything to do with this.

"Please, Sir if you were poisoned you would have felt the effects by now," Inspector Rashid tried to soothe him, "Now when was the last time you saw Mr Dale alive?" Inspector Rashid asked.

"I saw him while returning from the party. He was going towards his villa," Shyam said.

"What time was this?" Inspector Rashid looked at me and gave me his pen.

I guess I had to do the job of being the assistant in the absence of Inspector Hamid. I grabbed a notepad from the receptionist's desk and started taking down the conversation.

"Around 11.45pm. Like I said, we were on our way back from the party. Mr Dale was walking ahead of us. He couldn't even walk straight. Of course, at that time, I thought the old man was drunk. I did offer him my help, but he refused," Shyam said.

"And what about you, Mrs Kumar? Did you see anything unusual?" Inspector Rashid asked.

"No. I never spoke to the man. He was drunk, and he left the party early. That was the last time I saw him," She replied in a haughty tone and put her arm through her husband's.

"You didn't see him later walking ahead of you?" Mr Langhar asked.

"I was alone at that time. Ira's feet were hurting. I told her not to wear such high heels," Shyam corrected his statement hastily, "I called her a buggy, but I wanted to walk back."

"Who drove you back, Ira?" Mr Langhar asked.

"You are making me sound like a criminal Devin. All this interrogation! I don't know the name of every employee who works here," She said in an angry tone but then laughed out of nowhere. It was an attempt to hide her outburst, but it didn't fool anyone.

"What are you both doing here so early in the morning? Shouldn't you be enjoying breakfast," Inspector Rashid asked in a sweet voice.

"Oh, we came to inquire if the products got delivered on time. The resort's business is irreplaceable to us. And also to comment about the lax security," Shyam said.

"That was a load of BS," Inspector Rashid said as we left the manager's office, "The owner of a company coming to check whether the products are delivered? I don't believe that for a second."

"Yesterday I saw them talking to Mark Nettles. They looked friendly, and they had a long conversation. Today, however, Mr Nettles was acting as if he doesn't even know the Kumars beyond a business relationship," Mr Langhar said.

I saw a good opening for me to confess what I had overheard the night of the party.

"Yeah, I saw them too, Mr Langhar. They spoke for a while at the bar, and then the three of them went outside to the balcony. I was as surprised as you, Mr Langhar, because I thought Mr Nettles was going above and beyond common courtesy. Then I went to get a drink, and I actually overheard them talking. They were discussing something that was going to happen the night of the party," I said, fabricating a little and avoiding direct contact with the eyes of Inspector Rashid.

"What was going to happen?" Inspector Rashid squinted at me.

"They were planning something. Shyam wanted to change their plan, but Ira and Mr Nettles persuaded him to stick to the original plan," I replied, thinking back to the night. They had not discussed it out loud. But it was not innocent. Otherwise, the secrecy and today's lies were unnecessary.

Had Mr Dale seen something or heard something he was not meant to see or hear? And they had murdered him for that. Mr Dale was sitting near the bar when the three of them were talking. Maybe he overheard a part of their scheme. He was a blackmailer after all. His eyes were trained and practised to see things that ordinary people who minded their own business missed.

The fact of the matter was Shyam Kumar was the last person to have seen Jeffrey Dale alive. And he had a motive.

21

"This case is starting to tangle. Jeffrey Dale was seen walking on the beach at 11.00pm with a woman. Who could it be?" Inspector Rashid said.

"Noemie was at the party at that time, so we can exclude her. It could be Evelyn Miller or Estelle, Noemie Le Gall's daughter or Mrs Vyas. All three left the party before 11.00pm," I said.

"There's another way this crime could have been committed. Jeffrey Dale went back to his villa with this mystery woman. There would be no need to break-in. She could have simply walked in with her victim," Inspector Rashid said, "She strolls on the beach with Jeffrey Dale, convincing him that he was not in a state to manoeuvre his way back alone. Jeffrey Dale was intoxicated, out of his senses and judgment, and oblivious to his fate. She would have put him to bed, covering him with quilt, being a decent neighbour. And then waited for his victim to doze off, the perfect murder weapon waiting for her a few steps away."

"There is a flaw in that hypothesis. Shyam saw Jeffrey Dale entering his villa alone," Mr Langhar said, breaking my contemplation.

"He could be lying," I countered.

"Or..." Inspector Rashid said as another possibility occurred to him, "Let's not forget Noemie was the one who 'conveniently' toppled the whiskey glass of the victim. Maybe Mark Nettles is wrong about the time he saw Jeffrey Dale walking on the beach. It could have been later, after the party. And it was Noemie with the victim on the beach," Inspector Rashid said, "We can't exclude her."

I analyzed the words of Inspector Rashid. Estelle Le Gall was hiding something. That was an established fact. Would Jeffrey Dale blackmail a teenage girl? Or rather have enough dirt to blackmail her. I highly doubted that. But if I switched it up. It was Noemie Le Gall that was being blackmailed, and Estelle had aided her mother in killing a man. That would explain everything. I remembered the first day I had been in Noemie's presence. The revulsion I had experienced and the urge to run in the opposite direction. Noemie Le Gall was not innocent! And poison is a woman's murder weapon of choice. It gets the job done, and you don't need to be physically strong to get it done. If Mr Langhar was right, which he was, poison had been used not once but twice- phenobarbitone and then Insulin.

As we reached the boardwalk, our eyes were unsurprisingly drawn towards the beach. A bright red beach umbrella was standing tall, signalling the presence of guests on the shore.

"They are not going to be cooperative. You saw how reluctant the Dubai couple was. Devin, you should take the lead here," Inspector Rashid said, nodding towards the family from Paris spread out on the beach.

Mr Langhar nodded, and he and I descended down the wobbly staircase, this time on the northeast side of the property.

Noemie was lying face down on a beach towel outside the shade of the umbrella. She was wearing a skimpy yellow monokini, leaving nothing to imagination. She didn't fidget at the sound of our footsteps.

Raphael looked up, with a warm smile on his face. He was propped up on a pillow, reading a novel. Wearing a pair of white shorts, his thin torso was shirtless.

"Bonjour Reece, Devin," He said, closing his book.

"I hope we are not interrupting," Mr Langhar said. His tall figure was not a burden as he gracefully folded his legs under him and descended down on the sand.

"What kind of holiday it is if you don't make new friends," Raphael replied.

"I don't know if you have heard, but the police are considering Mr Dale's death suspicious," Mr Langhar said.

"He was killed?" Raphael said, using his hand in a slashing movement across his neck.

"Yes. When was the last time you saw him alive?" Mr Langhar asked.

"Oh, Devin! You don't need to be so formal, my friend," Raphael said, "Mr Dale left the party early if I remember, so then that was the last."

"And you, Noemie?" Mr Langhar prompted her.

"Who?" Noemie asked, raising her head. Her yellow sunglasses with white polka dots slid a little down the bridge of her sweaty nose.

"The man who died," Her husband replied.

"Who?" She asked again.

Raphael's face turned red, and I knew it was not because of the heat.

"The old man at the party," Mr Langhar said, trying to help her remember.

"He was wearing a brown coat," I added.

"Oh, that brown coat! It was ugly. And he had bad manners. Remember darling we were at the bar. He was listening to our conversation. And he didn't even try to hide it that he was eavesdropping," She launched into speech finally.

"I don't remember that. Anyways 'the assistant to the police' was asking when was the last time you saw Mr Dale alive?" Raphael said chuckling at the title he had invented for Mr Langhar.

I snickered helplessly at that only to get a death stare from Mr Langhar.

"Mark knows how to throw a party. I had such a good time. The music was amazing and the cocktails. Reece, you should dance more," She said and reverted to her sun tanning position.

Raphael sighed an apology for his wife.

"What are you doing here?" Estelle said, emerging from the water.

Raphael explained to his daughter our purpose in French, opening his novel simultaneously.

"Did you see anything, Estelle?" Mr Langhar inquired, observing her face.

"No. We are on holiday. You have no business interrupting our private time," Estelle said, her face swelling with anger.

Raphael said something to her rapidly in French, and she stormed off in the water again after glancing at her mother who lay oblivious to the above interaction.

"What did you do after the party?" Mr Langhar continued his line of questioning.

"Noemie wanted to stay at the party, but I was bored. I went for a walk after I left," Raphael said, "I should tell you this Devin. When I was walking on the beach, this very beach in fact- I saw Shyam standing in front of Jeffrey Dale's villa. I found it odd because his villa is next to mine on the opposite side. And now please excusez moi," He added and ignored us after that.

"I am glad the Inspector didn't come with us. We would have gotten nothing out of them," I said to Mr Langhar as we returned to his villa.

"What did Estelle ask you yesterday?"

"How did you know?" I asked astonished.

"She was trying to hide outside the villa that morning, not very successfully," Mr Langhar replied in his characteristic amused tone. He had a distinct charm when he spoke that way. It was like seldom he found things funny and when he did- he was a little surprised that he had found it hilarious.

"She was curious I guess, an ordinary adolescent curiosity," I said.

"If it were Jason, I would have agreed with you," He replied.

"Because she is a girl?"

"No, because she has inherited the self-centeredness from her mother. Why would she be interested in the death of an old man? That has nothing to do with her. It was odd

121

that she was lurking, trying to hear and see something that should not in anyways concern her."

"Okay, you are right. I was testing you," I said in awe of the man, "She was fishing for information and trying not to be transparent about it. I think she is involved somehow in this crime Mr Langhar."

"You were testing me?" Mr Langhar asked in a calm voice that scared me.

"No offence intended Mr Langhar. I wanted to test your knowledge of human psychology," I said, laughing to hide my discomfort and fear, "I am sorry," I added. I wanted to stay in the good books of the Indian detective.

He didn't reply, and we covered the remaining distance to his villa in silence.

22

The restaurant had opened its French windows tonight leading out to the balcony. Overlooking the black ocean, the balcony encircled the restaurant. Small round tables, covered with starched table cloths were spaced out to create a luxurious dining setting. The ornamental Himalayan salt lamps sitting on top were more for décor than for providing illumination, and Mr Langhar sitting across me was a silhouette.

The night air was warm on my face coming in waves like the water below us, ruffling my hair and stopping sweat from forming. It was peaceful in darkness, and I was beginning to breathe normally. I was not the prime suspect any longer.

Ignoring my monetary situation, I had ordered a glass of merlot and was now sipping it slowly, enjoying every drop. My companion was nursing a glass of scotch- the amber liquid glinting in the faint light of the Himalayan lamp.

Now was a good time as any other and I decided to open the Pandora's box before it was too late-

"Mr Langhar, I have to tell you something," I began.

"Yeah," He said, without changing his posture.

"I didn't want to mention this in front of Inspector Rashid..." I narrated the blackmail I had overheard, trying to stay as precise as possible; the words that had been said and what I had understood from listening between the lines. It was challenging to remember the words of a dead man now. He was a distant memory or a long-forgotten dream. His words and actions that had driven me crazy in the past seemed like they never took place.

But they had been real enough for the man or woman who had executed Jeffrey Dale, and for me.

"I cannot say who the other man was, but I can put my money that the one blackmailing was Jeffrey Dale," I finished.

"So he had found a victim here," He said in a distant voice, "You don't remember anything else?"

"No," I replied. The name that came to my mind was that of Norman Miller. But in light of the behaviour of Estelle Le Gall and even that of the Kumars and the manager, I couldn't take the name of Norman Miller.

Mr Langhar started to say something but a loud noise stopped him. Someone had pushed the wrought iron chair back, and the sound was loud as the legs screeched against the floor.

"Leave me alone. Why do you care what I do?" Estelle Le Gall's voice erupted in the darkness.

"All I am asking is an explanation," A man said in response.

"Why should I explain anything to you? You can go to the police if you want."

"I am not going to go to the police. Just tell me you didn't have anything to do with all this," The man said weakly.

"What if I did?" She spat at her receiver like a volcano spits lava with a vengeance. There was no response for that statement.

"Tell me why you took it," The man's said pleading after half a minute.

Estelle laughed, a cruel laugh and the sound of laughing grew fainter as she walked away.

"Who was the man?" I wondered.

"Can't you guess?" Mr Langhar replied, swirling his glass before taking a sip.

"Mr Langhar I think Estelle is involved in the murder. The way she is acting is suspicious, don't you think?" I said, giving up on guessing the identity of the man on the receiving end of her wrath.

"We don't have enough information to start making guesses."

"But haven't you formed a theory by now," I asked.

"Too many pieces, too many people. In my business, being hasty can be disastrous," He replied.

"You don't think Estelle's behaviour is worth following up?" I asked.

I simply didn't understand Mr Langhar. Estelle obviously knew something. If I were a detective, I would have cornered her and taken out every shred of information from her.

"If you want to talk about Estelle, you will have to talk about Jason- the Miller's son," He said unfazed.

"What about him?" I asked. The other teenager had barely registered on my radar.

"You didn't notice him on the beach this morning, when we were speaking to Le Gall's. He was there, hiding behind the trees. Why was he hiding? And why were he and Estelle arguing a moment ago?" He said.

"If we talk to one of them, then we can know what the other one is thinking," I said.

If Mr Langhar didn't think that teenagers could impart much knowledge, I was ready to interview them both myself. And the next time I got a chance; I was going to corner both Estelle and Jason.

"Hello to you both!" Om Vyas walked out to the balcony wearing yet again an outrageous outfit. Today he had opted for a brown cowboy jacket with long fringes hanging from the shoulder and the back. He had paired that with a black silk shirt and black pants. Mercifully he was not wearing cowboy boots.

Mrs Vyas standing next to him was looking as if she had descended from the royal family, sporting a beige dress. Om Vyas pulled a chair and sat down uninvited-

"What is this news about Jeffrey Dale being murdered, Devin?"

"It's the truth," Mr Langhar replied.

"How?"

"He was poisoned."

"With what?" Mrs Vyas asked, sitting down next to me.

"The police are not sure. You both were sitting at the same table. Did you see anything unusual?" Mr Langhar asked quickly.

"No," They both shook their heads.

"At any point during the evening, did anyone else come and sit at your table?"

"Well, Ira sat with us for a while, just before the showstopper performance. We have common friends in Mumbai," Mrs Vyas replied.

"And Mr Dale was sitting at the table at that time?"

"Yes, she occupied Reece's chair, next to Mr Dale. Are you helping the police?" Mrs Vyas asked.

"Unofficially. Did Jeffrey Dale leave his place during the evening?"

"He might have or might not have. I can't say. No, he did leave the table. I saw him with Norman outside in the balcony. They were smoking and talking," Om Vyas replied.

"When did Mr Dale start feeling queasy?" Mr Langhar asked.

"The showstopper performance was spectacular. What a marvellous performance! I wanted to congratulate T. Ted in person but...Anisha and I were focused on that. Only after the lights came back on, I realized that there was something wrong with Jeffrey Dale. That's when I alerted everyone in the room," Mr Vyas replied and then added, "I honestly thought he had too much to drink. They make strong drinks here, top-shelf stuff."

"You left my villa at around 2.30am if I remember right. Did you see anything or hear anything on your way back?"

"No Devin I was too tired! I didn't even change. I was asleep in seconds," Om Vyas replied, snapping his fingers to call a server.

23

"The plot thickens!" Inspector Rashid was bursting with animation when he entered Mr Langhar's villa the next morning. Pointing at the folder in his hand, he said, "Our victim was not a victim at all."

"I take it that you have confirmed that Jeffrey Dale was a blackmailer," Mr Langhar said coolly. His mild-temper may have deflated my enthusiasm, but Inspector Rashid knew his friend better.

Inspector Rashid continued in the same triumphant tone, "Yes. We got his bank account information, not an easy thing to acquire by the way. Jeffrey Dale was receiving money every month from one account. The bank won't disclose the sender, but they confirmed it was a private account. He has been getting the same amount for one year, and then last month he stopped getting that income."

"Most likely, he dried up his source. He was on the lookout for a fresh well and get this, he found one on this island," Mr Langhar said.

"You know more than us," Inspector Rashid said sulking.

Mr Langhar recounted the story of the blackmail briefly.

Inspector Rashid kept throwing dirty glances at me, and Inspector Hamid wrote everything down, as was his custom.

"And you have no idea who it was?" Inspector Rashid asked me incredulously.

"He was whispering. It's not like I know these people for years," I said equally incredulous at the insinuation that I should be able to recognize everyone's voice.

"Never mind that now. It proves that at least one person had a motive for murder. Reece, you told us that Jeffrey Dale had a newspaper back in the USA?" Mr Langhar asked me.

"Yes he used to run a newspaper in some city in Nevada, not Vegas, some small town and that's all I know," I said noticing Inspector Rashid's expression, "The newspaper shut down, however, some 25 years ago."

"Why?" Mr Langhar asked.

"I can tell you that," Inspector Hamid intercepted the conversation. His eyes glued to Mr Langhar's face he began, "Jeffrey's Dale newspaper was strictly local and notorious. It was infamous for putting gossip on the front page, gossips and scandals- whose wife was seen with whose husband, who spent a lot of time in the bathroom of a nightclub, things like that. I went through a couple of issues, and it was littered with such headlines. But Jeffrey Dale was smart to not name names. He added enough information, enough details, however, for a smart person to make accurate guesses about the identities," Inspector Hamid finished.

"I think that our 'victim' didn't develop his blackmailing habit after retirement. A serial blackmailer," Mr Langhar said a little disgusted, his thin nose crinkling in effect," Jeffrey Dale was in the perfect position to blackmail. The people who paid him stayed out of the front page and who didn't were hanged. Why did the newspaper shut down?"

"The newspaper published an article, and this one time Jeffrey Dale slipped. He published the name in bold letters. I don't know if it was intentional or an accident, but that story was accusatory, and it pointed the finger at an underage boy," Inspector Hamid said, "The authorities finally had enough evidence to shut down the paper. This was the article"

He handed over the newspaper cutting to us, printed on a piece of paper.

Murder Has No Age

Teen boy murders an innocent child. Authorities are turning a blind eye.

Perplexing states of events have developed in the case of the death of Michael Pike. Our readers will remember the unfortunate death by drowning of Michael (12) on the 24th of December.

Our small community was engulfed in horror at the senseless murder that the police has conveniently decided to call an accident.

Authorities questioned a suspect who was a close friend of Michael, a schoolboy of 14 years about the shocking incident. The people and this newspaper wonders why question friends or this particular friend at all if it was 'an accident'.

Our sources have now confirmed that there was severe animosity between the two boys, which the authorities are attributing to playful banter instead of savage rivalry.

A friend of Michael told us in confidence and at the condition of remaining anonymous, "Mike would have never

130

hung out with Mason Hall. He had no reason to be with him that afternoon. Mason Hall is a bully and Mike was scared of him. They were not friends."

This newspaper is concerned about the gross miscarriage of justice by ruling out the death as an accident instead of premeditated murder.

Young murderers are not that uncommon... continued on pg.5.

Below the article was a black and white picture of two boys. One was named Michael Pike (12) and the other Mason Hall (14).

"Is this allowed?" I asked.

"No, and that's why the newspaper was shut down. The locals started believing the story to be true and the 'Culprit's family had to leave the city for good," Inspector Hamid explained

"I think it is worthwhile asking Norman Miller about this. He is an American and 25 years ago he was a schoolboy," Inspector Rashid said.

What had inspector Rashid said- if it walks like a duck, talks like a duck, looks like a duck, then it is a duck. We were circling back to Norman Miller.

The first morning at breakfast, Norman Miller was flustered at the restaurant. If the boy in the newspaper article was Norman Miller then it explains why he was afraid of Jeffrey Dale.

"We can safely assume it was Norman Miller being blackmailed that night. Jeffrey Dale recognized him to be the boy who has killed before. Norman couldn't risk getting his past history out. He has a family now and by all evidence is extremely successful, *too much to lose.* Next morning conveniently, his villa got robbed. Of all the things that could have been taken, his anti-anxiety pills-the murder weapon got stolen. He was seen at the party, in the balcony talking alone to Jeffrey Dale, so he had the opportunity to slip the drug in his victim's glass. And the most damning piece of evidence, it was his tiepin found at the scene of crime. I asked around, he was wearing a suit that night. He wasn't wearing that tiepin during the party. Maybe he had with him and pocketed it before the party thinking it was too much for a casual gathering. It all adds up," Inspector Rashid laid the case before us.

"What do you say, Sir?" Inspector Hamid asked Mr Langhar.

"Let's talk to Norman Miller and his wife," Mr Langhar said in an absent tone. He was still gazing at the faxed paper with utmost concentration. Maybe this piece of evidence had finally convinced him.

Norman Miller had means, motive and opportunity.

24

We found Hassan sitting outside Mr Langhar's villa. He was picking apart a green palm leaf, tearing it painstakingly along its ridges. It was abnormal to see him sitting idle, his hands engaged in a fruitless activity.

"Good morning sir," He said to Mr Langhar, leaping to his feet and smoothening his wrinkle-less pants. He stood aside to let Inspector Rashid and Inspector Hamid pass him, the former glaring at him with suspicious eyes. But Hassan's dark eyes were fixed on Mr Langhar's face, relaying a message without saying a word.

"I will meet you at the Millers villa," Mr Langhar said to the Inspectors nodding once.

I was torn between staying with Mr Langhar or following the inspectors. I might miss something significant of their interrogation of the Millers. But then I did know, without Devin Langhar, the police rarely asked the right questions, and that made my decision.

"Excuse me, Sir, for stopping you. Is it true, Mr Dale was murdered?" Hassan broke into speech. He had waited patiently till the Inspectors were 50 yards away.

"Yes," Mr Langhar replied.

"I would talk to you and tell you everything than talk to the police. You know they blame us for anything that goes wrong," Hassan said and clamped up.

I agreed with that much.

"Were you at the boathouse party?" Mr Langhar asked, guiding him.

"No, sir."

"When was the last time you saw Mr Dale alive?"

"He called for the buggy in the evening. I drove him to the boathouse."

"Did he call you again after the party?" Mr Langhar asked.

"No sir," Hassan took a deep breath and launched into coherent speech, having gained enough self-assurance by the understanding behaviour of Mr Langhar-

"Sir, you should talk to Bhakti. She works in housekeeping. She knows something, Sir. She is so excited and happy. She is making plans for shopping, buying a new phone and going to India to see her family. It's not right, Sir, we make good money but not so much. Today she even failed to show up for work," He added the last line in anger.

I looked away, trying to hide my smile. The idea of an employee neglecting his/her duty was too much for Hassan to let go.

"Why was she excited? Did she say anything to you?" Mr Langhar asked.

"I don't want to get her in any trouble, but I think she killed Mr Dale," He said simply.

"What?" We both said out loud simultaneously.

"She showed me 2000 dollars, Sir. I don't know how she got so much money. I think she killed Mr Dale for money, Sir."

"You haven't seen her today?" Mr Langhar asked urgently.

"No. Bhakti was to come to work at 8.00am, but she didn't show up."

"Take me to where she lives. Reece go find the Inspector and meet us there," Mr Langhar said and pressed Hassan to move it.

I was confused at his urgency but decided not to question him. Was he scared that the housekeeper has made a run for it? She was shrewd enough. The image of Bhakti came to my mind. I had seen her only once, on the night of the party- making the blunder with the red wine. She had come across as a cunning woman and someone who would not mind shifting her morality to suit herself. If she murdered Mr Dale, 2000 dollars must be adequate.

My mind in a loop, I burst upon the inspectors in the Millers' villa.

"You have to come at once with me," I said with one foot out of the door.

"What's wrong?" Inspector Hamid asked.

"It's Mr Langhar- he wants you to follow him. Hassan said the housekeeper Bhakti is involved in the murder and Mr Langhar took off with Hassan to her house or wherever she lives," I said, my words tumbling out at random to convey the message in as few words as possible.

They got up immediately. The three of us were running rather than walking. The boardwalk creaked under our combined weight. We reached the restaurant when a buggy came rolling towards us, forcing us to flatten ourselves against an invisible wall. Inspector Rashid flagged the carriage to a stop and directed the driver to take us to the staff quarters.

The driver took us on a path lying on the right of the administrative building. The track ended in a large opening, at the end of which was three one-storey buildings arranged in a U-shape.

The door of the second room in the left-wing stood open, and the driver confirmed it was the Bhakti's room.

Hassan was standing outside. He was nervous, and he looked at the inspectors with fearful eyes.

Bhakti's room was small. There were no windows, and the solitary bulb over the door was switched on. Mr Langhar was sitting on the bed, and going through the articles of the drawer of the bedside table.

"Do you think she fled?" Inspector Rashid asked.

"I am afraid of a worse consequence," Mr Langhar replied.

Inspector Hamid gave orders to Hassan to locate the manager and bring him here.

The room was bare apart from the simple necessities. A single bed stood in the centre of the room with a low bedside table on its right. A plastic table was present next to the door. A cupboard with double doors occupied the corner next to the table. There were no pictures; no decoration and the walls were stark white.

"All her clothes are here," Inspector Hamid opened the cupboard.

"Look at this," Mr Langhar said, holding a cylindrical orange bottle in his hand, "It's the anti-anxiety pills."

"It's empty," I said.

"She killed Jeffrey Dale?" Inspector Rashid said, scratching the back of his neck, "But where is she?"

As if on a cue, Mark Nettles walked in.

"Do you know where Bhakti is?" Mr Langhar asked, standing up.

"No. Hassan she should be in your section."

"She didn't come for work today, Sir," Hassan replied.

"What..." Mr Nettles began, but Mr Langhar cut him short.

"Could she have gone to Malé or to any other island?" He asked.

"No. We didnt use any of the boats or the plane today. I can't say about yesterday," Mr Nettles looked at Hassan for an answer.

"She was at work yesterday, Sir," He replied.

"We need to look for the girl straight away," Mr Langhar said, but his voice was defeated.

25

None of the other members of the staff had seen the missing woman today. I was amazed that it took them so long to notice her missing. Considering how small this island was, I thought everyone would always be within breathing distance of each other.

But the fact was that the last time Bhakti was seen was yesterday at 10.30pm. Her neighbour had bid her goodnight, and that was the last sighting of the housekeeper.

She didn't leave the island- that much was certain. The only means to leave it was by the seaplane or by a boat and Mr Nettles was confident that none of those vehicles have been used.

Hence no one has left or arrived at the island since last evening.

Inspector Hamid assembled a search party, recruiting the staff members and dividing them into four search teams of three each. Nothing was said beyond we need to locate the missing girl.

We started the search from the main island. Every room of the staff compound was checked with no result. The search progressed in an outward fashion, and we probed the manager's office and the reception building with no answers. All the rooms were checked- even the locked rooms, much to the annoyance of the general manager.

"She couldn't possibly have ventured on into a locked room now- could she?" He said desperately, yanking out his master key once again to open a storage room located next to the welcome bar.

Some of the girls had given up hope when we started to look behind the 3-foot hedges lining the sandy path and soon after fearing the worst had given up the search. Some of the men had wanted to give up but prevailed, gulping down their ever-rising terror.

It was late afternoon by the time we completed the search on the main island, the private area having overwater villas and the associated beaches.

The sky had become progressively dark with grey clouds as the afternoon merged into evening, and the air grew colder. Nothing of the bright blue was left in the sky.

The sea had a life of its own now, and the waves crashed at the beach with a purpose. We retired into the safety of the palm trees and progressed towards our final destination.

The last place left to search was the part of the island where the boathouse was located and the property beyond it.

We walked through the tiny patch of the island jungle, a place where I encountered evil for the first time and which was most likely again at the centre of something terrible. But the forest floor was empty, devoid of any animal or human presence. The debris on the forest floor crunched under our feet as we reached the border and the boathouse came into view.

The building that gave the appearance of warmth and joy just two nights ago lay in darkness. There was no brightness of the string lights, no mellow music to blur the ominousness of the separate building. The six kayaks were there still, floating on the surface, but the waves were not gentle today. The 'thud' generated when a particularly strong wave hit the kayak and the kayak, in turn, made contact with the wooden pillar, was loud and menacing.

Mr Nettles' hand shook slightly as he inserted a key this time, without any protest in the door securing the entrance to the boathouse.

The stage was there, but the warm glow of the sunset was absent, and the white cover looked black against the grey sky outside.

I would never come here alone or even with two people, I thought. A shiver ran along my spine as I imagined what was waiting for us in the dark corners.

Mr Nettles flicked a light switch, and the room lit up dimly. To our temporary relief- it was vacant.

"Maybe one of our personnel is lying, and she did leave the island," Mr Nettles said, locking the door behind him.

Nobody believed him, and the search resumed onwards.

I had not come beyond this point, and another curve lay ahead of us. As we overcame that curve, a narrow beach with rocky formations on the edge of water came into view. Even in this grey weather, it looked striking, the waves crashing against the pointed stones and filling the small tide pools to the brim.

As we neared it, I understood why this spot was not commercialized. It was haunted. The shadow I had perceived on this island was present here, right now, looking down upon us. It was observing us and choosing who to give mercy and who to mark.

Two men were walking ahead of us. We saw them come to a halt at the top of a shallow rock; their faces telling the story of their discovery.

Inspector Rashid stopped the search party and nodded at Mr Langhar and me to follow him. We climbed carefully, navigating the needle rocks.

And then as I looked up to see how far we still have to go, I stopped short. My feet didn't want to go any further. I didn't need to go any further.

A woman's lifeless body was half inside the water and half behind the rock, hidden from anyone walking on the beach. She was wearing a dark blue dressing gown, and the black hair spiralled in the water like the head of Medusa.

Inspector Hamid bent down and turned her torso around, and wide-open, bloodshot eyes stared at the sky.

"It's Bhakti sir," One of the men who had found her said in a horrified whisper.

26

"She died last night, 16-18 hours ago. Cause of death-drowning," The police doctor was bent over the body, which was now lying on a black plastic sheet on the beach, face-side up.

"Did you examine her fingertips? She must have tried to fend off her attacker?" Mr Langhar asked.

"Yes. Didn't find anything, didn't expect to find anything. Water has been lapping around her continuously, wave after wave washing over her. The hair and the gown are still wet. Even if she managed to scratch or grab her attacker, all the evidence is gone by now. But I will check for it, and I will comb her clothes at the lab but don't count on that evidence," The doctor replied.

There was nothing more to do for us. Inspector Hamid had dispersed the search team. Mark Nettles, defeated, had followed the tiny horde back to the main island.

"Why was she killed?" I said, "She got her money! She would have kept quiet. Isn't this too big a risk?"

"Not when the killer has a chance of being caught. The killer won't leave any loose ends, and no risk is big," Mr Langhar said, "Hassan told me that she showed him 2000 dollars. But we didn't see any trace of it in her room. The killer must have taken it back knowing we could trace the bill," Mr Langhar added.

Devin Langhar had retreated back into his shell after the discovery of the body. The difference now was that instead of a tranquil, confident expression, his face radiated unwavering concentration.

"But Mr Langhar they were American dollars. The killer is Norman Miller. Every evidence points to him," Inspector Hamid said.

"This resort only accepts American dollars. That's not a good pointer. But you are right- let's go pick up where we left," Mr Langhar said.

After the primitive darkness of the beach, it was a relief to step onto the dimly lighted boardwalk. The restaurant was in business, and as we crossed it, the sound of music reached us, followed by a loud laugh. The balcony dining was closed today, and we passed unspotted and uninterrupted.

Eventually, we reached the last villa on the east side, the plaque outside displaying the name 'Emerald'.

"Mr Miller, please take a seat," Inspector Rashid had bustled in without ceremony and now pointed at a chair in the living room for Norman to sit down.

"What's the meaning of this? You do know the time Inspector," Norman Miller was red-faced.

By the looks of it, the Millers were heading out for dinner. Inspector Hamid had locked Evelyn Miller in the master bedroom, but their son Jason was nowhere to be seen.

"We neglect time in matter of emergency. A woman has been killed," Inspector Rashid said.

"What?" Norman Miller sank in the chair.

"She was the housekeeper- Bhakti," Mr Langhar said.

"Oh, we have Jackson handling our villa. I don't know her."

"So you have never met her?" Inspector Rashid pounced.

"I met her once. She was snooping in our villa. Let me tell you- very suspicious. She said she was cleaning our villa because Jackson was busy. Well, I didn't question it. But as she was leaving, I noticed she didn't have any cleaning supplies with her. I mentioned it to Evelyn, my wife that we should make sure all our valuables are locked. How did she die?"

"She was drowned," Inspector Rashid said.

Norman Miller closed his eyes and covered them with his hands.

"When did the robbery take place?" Mr Langhar asked.

"The night before the boathouse party. Considering all the things that have been happening in this resort, I am glad all we had to endure was a robbery," Norman Miller said, his hands still over his eyes. Was it because he was too overcome with horror or was he trying to hide his eyes and his face, lest the Indian detective read his false expressions?

"You noticed the medicine missing when?" Mr Langhar asked.

"That night. I went to take it before sleeping, but the bottle was missing," Norman replied.

"But it could have been stolen anytime in the past 24 hours," Mr Langhar stated.

"I didn't think of that. You are right- I just noticed it missing in the night. I assumed someone might have come in and nicked it when we were out for dinner. Why is this important now? The police didn't bother showing up when we first reported the crime?" Norman said, squinting at Inspector Rashid.

"You didn't report the crime," Inspector Rashid said, menace in his voice.

"Is this your pill bottle?" Inspector Hamid raised the transparent plastic packet containing the bottle.

"Yes. Where did you find it?"

"We have reason to believe that your prescription medicine were used on Jeffrey Dale," Inspector Rashid said, raising a finger to stop Norman from speaking, "Now think carefully back to the night of the party Mr Miller. When was the last time you saw Jeffrey Dale alive?"

"When he left the party. He was the first one to leave. Where did you find the bottle?"

"Witnesses place you talking to him during the party. Did you know him from before?" Inspector Rashid said, ignoring Norman Miller's question.

"No, I have never met him before. I went out for a smoke before the showstopper performance, and the old man followed me out to the porch."

"What did you talk about?" Inspector Rashid asked.

"Nothing in particular- weather and politics- he was an American citizen. But I didn't particularly like him, so I kept the conversation short."

"What time did you leave the party?" Inspector Rashid asked.

"Around 11.30am. My wife and I left together."

"What did you do after that?" Inspector Rashid asked.

"We went back to our villa. Why are you talking to me in that tone?" Norman Miller roared.

"One more question Norman, how will anyone know that you have anti-anxiety medicine in your room. Who did you tell about it?" Mr Langhar asked.

I looked at the Indian detective in amazement, and I was not the only one. Inspector Rashid was staring at him with the same expression. His ability to analyze and not get sidetracked with apparently more appealing evidence was supernatural.

"Anyone could have known," Norman said after thinking for 30 seconds, "We were at breakfast that morning, the morning of the robbery. I was feeling rattled. My wife and I had gone scuba diving, and a close encounter with a shark had left me in quite a shock. I said, and anyone could have heard- where did you keep my anti-anxiety pills? You see, I didn't have any reason to keep my voice low."

"Who all were in the room?" Mr Langhar asked.

"Besides you, Reece and Jeffrey Dale- all the other guests staying around us."

"Have you seen this before?" Inspector Hamid pulled out another plastic bag from his pocket.

"It's my tiepin. Where did you find it?" Mr Miller jumped up.

"Was this stolen as well?" Inspector Rashid asked, cracking a sideways smile.

"Yes. I left it on the bathroom counter, and the next day it was not there. Where did you find it?" Mr Miller said, his red face perspiring in full force.

It was difficult to imagine Norman Miller as a person who murdered two people in a cold-blooded manner. His troubles with anxiety, his defeated posture- everything made him more of a victim than a killer.

"That's all for now," Inspector Rashid said and pocketed the tiepin.

Evelyn Miller replaced her husband in the chair. She was more poised than Norman at the sudden interrogation. Dressed in a white dress, she sat with her legs crossed.

"This is highly inappropriate," She said, her eyes on Mr Langhar as if he was the only one who would be expected to understand social propriety.

"Another death has occurred. One of the housekeeper-Bhakti has been murdered," Mr Langhar lead the questioning "But we must talk about the night of the boathouse party Mrs Miller."

"Please call me Evelyn. I wish I could help you, but I never spoke to the man."

"Do you remember anything unusual?"

"No everyone was enjoying themselves. I was enjoying myself- I really didn't pay attention to other people, most of all, Mr Dale."

"What time did you leave the party?" Mr Langhar asked.

"At 11.30pm. Me and Norman left together."

"Now, about the robbery. Your husband said that he found Bhakti inside your villa when usually Jackson cleans it?" Mr Langhar said.

"Yes, in fact, I was the one who pointed out that to Norman. He doesn't have much observation power for these kinds of details or any detail as a matter of fact. Did he mention she didn't have any cleaning supplies with her? Oh well, I always make it a point to lock all the valuables in the safe whenever I am staying in a hotel- you can never be too careful. The poor girl might have nicked a few loose dollars at the most."

"Could she have nicked the anti-anxiety pills?" Mr Langhar said, his voice sharp.

Evelyn didn't speak for a minute. She was chewing her lower lip, looking at Mr Langhar's face.

"She might have," Evelyn Miller got up slowly and stopped at the door.

"You know I might as well add this- I saw Shyam standing outside Mr Dale's villa at around 11.45pm. I was pulling the window shade down- it becomes unbelievably bright in the morning, and he was standing there looking out at sea. I found it extremely bizarre."

"Was anyone else with him?" Mr Langhar asked.

"No he was alone," She said and with a last glare, left the living room leaving us to show ourselves out.

27

"Hamid and I will go to Malé to get the warrant for arrest. Please keep an eye on them," Inspector Rashid said and left us for the night.

Mr Langhar looked at their retreating figure until they were out of sight. Then he made his way speedily towards the villa 'Jade'.

The yellow tape was wrapped around the round knobs, prohibiting entrance, loose ends flapping in the wind, and in effect providing an auditory warning as well as a visual one. But we found the door unlocked.

The Indian detective stood at the threshold for an instant, his face focused. He then walked inside and closing the distance in two long strides he paused again at the junction that led to the bedrooms, the door on the left was my old bedroom, and the one on the right was the master suite.

I didn't want to say anything to disturb his thoughts, and hence I just followed him as he after another instant of pausing turned right and pushed the master bedroom door open. He stopped at the threshold again. After what seemed like forever, he walked towards the foot end of the bed. A small suitcase was on top of the bench.

"What are you looking for?" I couldn't keep quiet any longer.

"This is Jeffrey Dale's carry-on case?" He asked me.

"Yes."

He made me stand at the entrance, not trusting me to help him in the search. He went through the contents of the suitcase meticulously and then straightened up, obvious disappointment written on his face.

"The police has searched his room already Mr Langhar," I reminded him.

He ignored me like before and progressed to the bedside table and opened the drawer. He pulled out a syringe with its cover and placed it on the top of the table.

"He always kept his needles there," I said, "Be it at home or at a hotel."

Mr Langhar didn't say a word and moved to the writing desk and opened the single long drawer. He lifted a magazine out this time.

"Oh, he had it all along," I said, rolling my eyes.

"What?" Mr Langhar asked.

"He purchased that magazine at Heathrow. At the party, he made a big fuss about how I had misplaced it, and he wants it a.s.a.p. It's a magazine for crying out loud," I said. It was silly of me to get angry with a dead man, but the embarrassment of the night came rushing back, and the resentment rose up inside me. Right at this moment, I was not sorry that Jeffrey Dale was dead.

Mr Langhar started flipping through the magazine one page at a time. I sighed loudly but to no effect.

I had taken a step towards the bed when Mr Langhar uttered aloud, "Ha."

His index finger was pointing at an article, and he passed the magazine to me.

The masterminds have fled the country

The regulations and the legal repercussions seem to have no effect in admonishing the masterminds of Wall Street. Another such case in a history dotted with frauds has struck the New Yorkers and investors beyond.

Jared Bailey and Karen Bailey are the new Bonnie and Clyde to have robbed the country and successfully fled the scene.

The authorities are more baffled about their successful escape than how the fraud was committed.

I wanted to read further, but the photograph under the article drew my eyes. The faces looking out from the pages were that of Norman and Evelyn Miller.

"They are going to get caught because they failed to remove a silly magazine," I said slowly.

"Most of the time, a killer is caught because they have made a stupid mistake or the criminals were arrogant in thinking the police won't notice those details. And then we catch them," Mr Langhar replied.

"But you don't think so in this case," I asked, catching the caution in his tone.

Devin Langhar was a cautious man and not afraid to be slow. Where another may start babbling in the face of excitement and sudden discovery, Mr Langhar stopped short and checked himself. It could be frustrating for a person who didn't have the patience to deal with his genius- like Inspector Rashid but once you began to see Mr Langhar's brilliance and his method you know that he takes his time, but once he is sure, he can never be wrong. And Devin Langhar was not sure right now.

"That's too obvious a mistake," He said.

28

A spluttering and screaming nozzle was the noise overwhelming my morning when the doorbell rang.

"Got the warrant. Do you want to be there when we arrest the Millers?" Inspector Rashid said joyfully.

Mr Langhar nodded. He had called the Inspector last night after he had unearthed the damning article. The warrant was now for both Mr and Mrs Miller.

Two constables were standing outside the American villa.

"They are inside, sir," One of them told the Inspector.

It would have been uncomfortable to watch if I wasn't aware of the crimes committed by the people inside- cold-blooded murder of two people.

Om Vyas had stumbled out from his villa and was now walking briskly towards us. Behind him, Mrs Vyas was putting her hair in a ponytail and walking at the same time.

Norman Miller opened the door clad in the white terry gown of the resort. His expression turned from annoyance, to surprise, to fear rapidly. He fell back a step, and Inspector Rashid entered the villa with his backup.

Mr Langhar's mouth was a thin line, and he didn't follow the Inspector inside. Hence I was obligated to stay out of the actual arrest as well. Did he still not believe that the Millers had done the murders?

After what seemed like minutes, the husband and the wife were led out- handcuffed. The police had obliged

Norman Miller, and he was wearing jeans and a t-shirt. He seemed resigned to his fate, head hanging low and shoulders bent, walking with tired steps. His son Jason walked out behind them free from any physical chains. I felt sorry for him at least.

But Evelyn Miller was spitting fire-

"You can't pin these murders on us. We have no reason to kill that old man or that woman. You can't make a scapegoat of us inspector. Why will we kill them?" She said.

"Because he was blackmailing you both. We know all about it, Mrs Miller or should I call you Mrs Bailey? We know everything! How you escaped America with stolen money. Jeffrey Dale found out about it, and he had to be silenced," Inspector Rashid said, strutting and looking around at the assembled audience.

"Those are white-collar crimes you baboon. Do you really think we are that dumb? To kill a man?" She was shouting with all she had.

"So you admit he was blackmailing you?" Inspector Rashid pounced.

"Yes. I don't know how Jeffrey Dale found out, but he blackmailed us. And I was relieved when somebody else took care of that problem for us. But we didn't kill him," Norman Miller said in a small voice.

"But I know something you don't know Inspector. Jeffrey Dale was blackmailing others at this resort. He told me as much when he was extorting money from us the night of the party. He said he would have never imagined that such a small group of people could provide him with so much opportunity," Evelyn Miller said.

"Okay, that's enough," Inspector Rashid said, "We will talk at the police station."

In the five minutes that it had taken the Maldivian Police force to arrest the infamous Americans, the entire guest list had assembled outside the Millers villa. Inspector Hamid had to stay behind, and he tried to scatter the audience.

"Now we don't have to live in fear," Raphael bowed in the direction of Inspector Hamid, "Do the Police owe their rapid success to you, Devin?"

Mr Langhar shrugged his shoulder in response.

My eyes, however, were fixated on Estelle Le Gall. She was standing behind her mother, her right hand on her mother's shoulder. And she was ecstatic. Her face radiated exorbitant relief as if she had taken a full breath of air for the first time.

The last sentence, Evelyn Miller, had said, came back to me. *He told me as much when he was extorting money from us the night of the party. He said he would have never imagined that such a small group of people could provide him with so much opportunity.* Were Estelle and her mother one of them?

"I always knew it was Norman Miller. There was something in his eyes that made me suspect he was disturbed. He was stressed out all the time- sweating and shuffling. But his wife to be in on it, such a homely woman, that was a shock to me," Om Vyas said.

"She was the mastermind," Mr Langhar said.

"Mrs Miller?" I said, "I am sure her husband was the one who planned everything, and she got dragged alongside him."

"You don't need to talk to be in charge," Mr Langhar said curtly.

Mrs Vyas nodded at Mr Langhar.

"Shyam was telling us he saw a woman with Jeffrey Dale the night of his murder. It must have been Evelyn, correct Shyam?" She turned her head to locate the subject of her statement, but there was no sign of either Shyam or Ira.

29

"They are not here," Noemie asked, looking around.

"Weren't they standing with us?" Mrs Vyas said.

"Actually I haven't seen them," I said. I had assumed that everyone was present to witness the morning show.

Mr Langhar stared at us for a second and then took long strides towards the Kumar's villa. Inspector Hamid and all of us rushed behind him.

The Kumar's villa was the last one on the east side, near the restaurant. It was unnaturally silent. The shades were down, and the light bulb outside was still glowing.

Mr Langhar knocked at the door, hastily, "Has anyone seen them today?"

Getting a negative response, Hassan was directed to open the door.

"I can feel something is wrong," Mrs Vyas said as Mr Langhar and Inspector Hamid disappeared inside.

"Why would the Americans kill them?" Raphael wondered.

It was unimaginable that two more people were lying dead somewhere on the island. The assurance that had come with the arrest of the Millers was shattered like a mirror.

"There's no one inside," Mr Langhar said, walking towards us.

"Sir, I must alert the Inspector," Inspector Hamid said.

We found Inspector Rashid in conversation with Mark Nettles. They were standing at the dock, waiting for the ferry to come back and take the Inspectors to the seaplane.

"Sir, we have a situation. The Kumars are not in their villa," Inspector Hamid said.

"What?" The senior Inspector whipping his head, "Do you think something has happened to them?" He asked Mr Langhar.

"Mr Nettles I want you to take an inventory of your boats, your scooters, your scuba gear and frankly anything that might help someone leave this island," Mr Langhar gave instructions to the manager.

"Surely you are not suggesting they tried to get away on a scooter or a kayak?" Inspector Rashid said, laughing out loud, "How far could they go? This resort can only be accessed via seaplanes. Besides, why would they run?"

Mr Langhar didn't reply immediately, watching the retreating figure of the manager. Then he said, "All I know is that two people cannot escape this island without a little help from people on this island."

"So you think they ran off, but why? The Millers have already killed two people. What's two more lives for them?" Inspector Rashid said, jerking his head towards the seaplane.

"I will meet you at the Kumar's Villa," Mr Langhar said succinctly and motioned me to follow him.

"Where are we going?" I asked.

"This way," He walked a lot faster than I, his long legs contributing to his speed. I had to semi-jog to keep up with his 6 feet frame.

It became clear where we were heading as the administrative building came into sight. But Mr Langhar, instead of going through the front doors, kept walking and took the path to the staff quarters. Then he took a left turn, and the backside of the administrative building came in to view.

The rear was devoid of windows, but there was a door with chipping brown paint. It must be an emergency exit.

Mr Langhar turned the knob gently and pushed the door slightly inwards. The secretary was absent from her desk, and we crept inside.

"There was a bathroom attached to the manager's office. It must be a common restroom," Mr Langhar whispered, pointing at the door behind the receptionist's desk.

"Are you going to break into Mr Nettles office?" I asked. I dared not ask why we were here after the dirty glance Mr Langhar threw at me in response to the first question.

I tried the knob this time, and it was unlocked. As Mr Langhar had predicted, it was a restroom. The door leading to Mr Nettles' office was ajar, and we both shuffled silently towards it.

"I thought he was going to check up on Kayaks and whatnot," I whispered, baffled to find the manager in his office. Mr Langhar put a finger to his lips as a warning.

Mark Nettles was sitting in his chair, dialling a number on his desk phone.

"How far have you reached?" He said after a few seconds, "You must make it to the airport to catch the flight, any flight out of here at once," He paused again,

"I think we are fine. I am going to persuade the police to organize a search party for you. That should buy us some more time. Devin Langhar thinks you have escaped by the sea and the Inspectors think you are dead. Of course, no one will believe Mr Langhar. The police think it is absurd to imagine you leaving by the sea. Besides you don't have any reason to run," Mark Nettles gave a nasty laugh.

He listened for a bit and then added, "Don't worry, I will take care of it. It's safe."

He put the receiver down and hurriedly left the room.

"What does all this mean?" I said pronouncing each word carefully.

"He helped Shyam and Ira escape from the island," Mr Langhar replied.

"So that means these three killed Jeffrey Dale and that poor woman and not the Millers," I said stunned.

30

"You are back," Inspector Rashid said. He was standing in the living room of the Kumars' abandoned villa. The glass deck doors were open, and the east-facing villa was full with morning light.

"What did you find?" Mr Langhar asked.

"You are right. The Kumars left in a hurry. Some clothes are gone. The shoes have been left behind, and so are the toiletries. They packed one suitcase and left the remainder of the luggage behind," Inspector Rashid said, walking through the bedroom and leading us into the dressing room.

Two suitcases were resting on low marble benches with some paraphernalia inside. The dresser drawers were open. Black felt lined hangers were on the floor instead of their usual place on the metal rod. The coat that Shyam wore on the night of the boathouse party was in a bundle on the floor.

Inspector Hamid walked in with a man wearing the uniform of the resort.

"This is Jackson. He is the host for villas on the east side. He noticed the suitcase was missing Sir," Inspector Hamid said.

"How do you know so well about their luggage?" Inspector Rashid asked.

"They are frequent guests here, Sir. I always attend to their needs. That's why I know that they had another small suitcase with them," Jackson replied. This time I could detect an Australian accent clearly, and his physique matched his accent.

"Does Mr Nettles know the Kumars well?" Mr Langhar asked.

"They are good friends, Sir," He replied.

Jackson was dismissed after revealing that piece of information.

"They knew each other well, after all. Why was the manager lying?" Inspector Rashid said.

"That's not the only thing he is lying about," Mr Langhar began telling him about the phone conversation we had overheard, but before he could elaborate, Mark Nettles walked in.

"You were right Devin. Two of our kayaks are missing. I can't imagine our staff being so careless. Be assured the person responsible for this negligence will not be spared. Did they steal stuff from the villa?" He said. His eyes were shifting from left to right as he read the faces of the people in the dressing room.

"Was there anything worth stealing?" Mr Langhar asked in a low tone.

"Not really. We hope the guests staying here have hopefully got towels at home," Mr Nettles replied, laughing.

"Very funny," Inspector Rashid said instead of laughing.

Mr Langhar slipped outside. He was in searching mode again. Just like the day he had discovered the magazine, he began prodding each inch of the villa. He was like a bloodhound. If there were anything worth finding, Mr Langhar would find it.

He started with the bathroom. He checked the cupboards under the double sink, behind the laundry basket and finding nothing moved to the bedroom. Mr Langhar went methodically through the dresser in the bedroom and the two bedside tables.

A look of confusion coloured his face as he peered into the waste paper basket. He unwrapped his handkerchief and pulled a shampoo bottle from the pit of the dustbin.

"Why is this in the bedroom?" Mr Langhar said, examining the empty shampoo bottle.

I looked at the Inspectors to get a hint of Mr Langhar's curiosity. It was an empty bottle; it was where it was supposed to be, in the waste paper basket.

"It's a shampoo bottle," Mr Nettles said. And to my amazement sweat beads had materialized on his forehead.

"Why will they carry their own shampoo?" Mr Langhar said, looking in the manager's eye.

"Devin many of our guests carry their own kits. It is comfortable and known to them," Mr Nettles replied, cracking a broken smile.

"Isn't it time to give up the game Mr Nettles?" Devin Langhar said in a quiet voice. He looked at the face of the manager for a long time before speaking to the senior Inspector, "Rashid alert the airport authority to be on the lookout for the Kumars. While you are at it arrest Mark Nettles. I know what this is all about."

31

Inspector Rashid, dressed in his official police uniform, looked as if he was the sole possessor of the key to the gates of heaven. He was trying not to smile, though the corners of his mouth were farther apart than I remembered. His eyes couldn't contain the triumph that engulfed him, and they were twinkling with delight.

A handful of reporters encircled the podium, their spotlights setting the face of Inspector Rashid ablaze.

The remaining guests had assembled in the restaurant, and the 66-inch TV was fired up for the special telecast.

There was Mr and Mrs Vyas seated together, nearest to the TV. The adventures had taken a toll on the dressing sense of Om Vyas and today he was wearing a brown polo t-shirt and black pants.

Then there was the French family huddled together at the far end of the table, their eyes transfixed on the television. Estelle was holding her mother's hand tightly over the table.

Hassan was standing near the Television holding the remote and Jackson was sitting near the entrance.

My mind travelled back to the first day here. My subconsciousness had picked up something eerie back when the façade of perfection and tranquillity was still in place. The 'It' had a presence among us then. It was living and breathing, choosing who to mark and who to spare; deciding whether to bestow mercy or separate the gut from the body. But 'It' had done its damage and two lives had been claimed.

Inspector Rashid began speaking, and I breathed a sigh of relief. Everything was peaceful now.

"This particular crime ring had been operating for the past year. The Maldivian Police always stay on alert for possible drug infiltration. Holiday destinations and criminals are a match made in heaven. These criminals tried to cast their web in our country as well. They had been operating as I said for a year now. We were monitoring the situation closely, and we did manage to catch a few peripheral players. Still, we never reached the centre of the web."

"Mark Nettles, Shyam Kumar and Ira Kumar have been smuggling several illicit drugs in bottles labelled as shampoos, conditioners and lotions. The criminals keep coming up with new ways to smuggle illegal drugs, but as always, the Police were one step ahead. Today we have caught the criminals, or I should say the biggest players. I would like to extend my sincere thanks to the excellent work of my esteemed friend- Devin Langhar. He was pivotal in catching the criminals, and we could only thank our stars that he was present at the right place to curtail this situation. Thank you," Inspector Rashid concluded his statement.

Mr Langhar suddenly got interested in the contents of the coffee cup he was holding.

"You should be proud of your talent Devin," Mrs Vyas said, patting his shoulder, "Drug smuggling! They looked so decent. I even invited them to visit us when they come to Mumbai," Mrs Vyas added, shaking her head.

"How did they smuggle the drugs?" Raphael asked.

"The drugs were filled in shampoo and conditioner bottles and shipped with the bottles having actual products. The cartons having the drugs were carefully labelled to segregate them from the rest of the stock. The Kumars used to hand-deliver the shipment for they couldn't afford to trust anyone. Mark Nettles used to personally receive the shipment at this end. They succeeded in staying hidden for so long because they didn't trust anyone outside the three of them."

"It was easy work after that. The next stage was distributing the drugs in Maldives. But before that, they had to find a place to store their supply. They couldn't risk storing the drugs in a villa or a room on the island. What if a guest or an employee accidentally stumbled upon it? So the three of them came up with another ingenious solution. The villa 'Jade' was chosen to hide their supply. It was the perfect plan. The drugs were emptied from the bottles and wrapped up in waterproof packaging. Then they would attach the drugs under the villa where it remained hidden and safe."

"This time though an error happened. Jeffrey Dale was assigned the villa 'Jade'. So a new plan had to be concocted. A boathouse party was put together. The guests from the surrounding villas will be at the party, and the smugglers would have no chances of being spotted."

"But even the best-laid plans go wrong. Shyam had the job of keeping a lookout while Ira swam and unloaded the drugs, sticking it under Jeffrey Dale's villa."

"Why didn't they just put the drugs under their own villa?" Raphael asked.

"Changing the location of the drugs would have been suicide for their business. They would have to make contact with the other members of the gang. Remember they were undetected because no one knew who they were," Mr Langhar explained.

"And Mr Dale saw them? That's why he was killed? He reached his villa earlier than they anticipated," I asked.

The Police had sent divers first under the Kumar's villa, but nothing had been found. Then Mr Langhar had the brilliant insight of checking under my old villa, and we had hit the jackpot. After we had retrieved the drugs, Mark Nettles had fallen apart and confessed to drug trafficking.

"They didn't mention anything about the arrest of the Millers?" Estelle said before Mr Langhar could answer.

"The Kumars and Mark Nettles are charged with drug trafficking, and the Millers are shipped back to USA for fraud," Mr Langhar said.

"What about the murders? Two people died," Om Vyas said.

"The killer has been enormously lucky. So many smokescreens to hide behind and disappear in the chaos. But the time has come to close the final chapter, the chapter illustrating the heinous crime committed on this island- not one but two murders," Mr Langhar said. His voice was impassive, but it was powerful, and the hair at the back of my neck stood up.

The silence was so profound that all I could hear was of the waves. Mr Langhar's words didn't make any sense.

"I have been involved in many cases, some very complex cases which have been relatively straightforward to solve and some very simple cases which have been the most difficult in my career. This case I will remember for this reason- the number of criminals I encountered in such a small group of people."

"The crime was a crime of desperation. But at the same time, our murderer was careful about not making a mistake. Desperate times lead to desperate measures, and the law enforcement hopes that a desperate criminal will act irrationally, hastily, without thinking and therefore make mistakes."

"The crucial question was – what's the motive? Here was a group of people who have never met each other. No connection is apparent at the surface. One family is from London, another from New York, one from Paris, one from Dubai and of course from India," Mr Langhar said, "Why will anyone want to kill a man they apparently didn't even know?"

"The motive became clear when we checked the villa of the dead man. Jeffrey Dale preyed upon people he knew won't strike against him. People who had a lot to lose and thought that paying was a better solution than coming face to face with their secrets."

"But this time Jeffrey Dale judged one person wrong. A serial blackmailer by profession blackmailed the wrong person. This time, to put it simply, he made a lethal enemy."

"The killer chose the night of the boathouse party as the right time. Anyone could have done it. Everyone present at the party had ample opportunity to poison the glass of Jeffrey Dale. And it was easy- in the hustle and noise of the party no one was paying attention."

"At first, we were led to believe that it was an impulsive act. The murderer had enough and decided to be quick about it before the adrenaline rush passed and reason took over. It was a quick and easy method to kill. The murderer put the anti-anxiety pills in Jeffrey Dale's glass and voila- it was done. But before the murderer could feast on the completion of the act and take a breath of relief- Jeffrey Dale left the party- *alive*."

"The murderer couldn't take that chance. Making sure of his death was necessary; for if he lived to tell the tale- our killer would be ruined. And here we witness the patience of our killer. We get the proof the murderer has done it before."

"The murderer waited for the party to end and then went to Jeffrey Dale's villa in the dead of night. The killer swam and reached the villa. It was too risky to come through the front door. It was child's play to open the back door and check if the original plan had gone to fruition. The sound of shallow breathing was an inconvenience at the most. It was the easiest thing in the world to creak the refrigerator open and procure another weapon to fulfil the aim. The insulin did the job what the anti-anxiety pills could not. Jeffrey Dale would not pose a problem anymore. The murderer was safe now."

"Imagine the horror the killer must have experienced when the housekeeper Bhakti put two and two together. She had stolen the anti-anxiety pills from the Miller's villa for a small price. But like a cunning but short-sighted person who only sees the next 10 steps in front of her, she decided to ask for more money, not realizing that she was signing her death certificate. Two people have blackmailed a killer now, and she met the same fate as Jeffrey Dale."

"You can imagine what would have happened. The woman called away from prying eyes to the haunted waters; her triumphant giddiness at her intelligence and good sense to extract as much honey as possible. The killer was waiting for her. It was time to tighten up the loose ends. She got a painful death instead of more money. The housekeeper made the same mistake that Jeffrey Dale did-targeted the wrong person."

"Surely you knew you couldn't escape a second time Raphael or should I address you by your real name Mason Hall," Devin Langhar said zeroing in on the charming Parisian man.

32

"I assure you Monsieur Langhar I have one name," Raphael Le Gall said, an amused smile on his lips.

"You are the killer. You have all the makings of one. I am sure no one in this room besides me would have even suspected you. Who would suspect a man, who lives in the shadow of his wife? I congratulate you on procuring such an effective camouflage," Mr Langhar replied.

"I do not appreciate your baseless accusations. If you have any proof, I am all ears. But if you are going to talk from the top of your head, I have somewhere better to be. What motive do I have to kill that old man?" Raphael said, standing up, his voice getting louder with each word.

"Blackmail," Mr Langhar said quietly, "Jeffrey Dale was blackmailing you."

"All my business dealings are per the law. I don't have skeletons in my closet. What will he blackmail me with?" Raphael said coldly.

"Sure your record has been spotless in France. But what about the time you were residing in America?"

"I have never been to America," Raphael snarled.

"It's fairly easy to obtain information when you know where to dig. The case was puzzling. What motive could a person have against someone he or she was supposedly meeting for the first time? But in the end, it turned out to be straightforward- he was not meeting the victim for the first time," Mr Langhar said.

"This story had its roots embedded in the soil of America when you Mason Hall first crossed paths with Jeffrey Dale. The boy who drowned didn't die by accident-you killed him deliberately. Jeffrey Dale printed the story, and your family was forced to run back to France. It was sheer coincidence when after all these years you laid eyes on the man who suspected you back then. You were scared that the hornet's nest would be kicked once more."

"I am sure you thought Jeffrey Dale won't even recognize you. It was all so long ago. You are a grown man with a family and distinctly French. Surely he won't recognize you! But you never realized the distinguishing feature of your physical self would be enough for Jeffrey Dale to identify you. The scar on your right forearm," Mr Langhar said, pointing at it.

Raphael's left hand in reflex covered the scar but not before we saw the white scars. They looked like slanted raindrops, pale against his skin.

"That's how he recognized you. That's how I recognized you," Mr Langhar finished.

Raphael only had eyes for Mr Langhar, and he stared at the Indian detective with angry eyes. Then he broke into speech-

"He had the guts after what he had done to come again for me," Raphael spat out the words in perfect English, all hints of an accent gone, "I was too young back then to take care of him. I was forced to obey my parents and run like a coward. But this time I wasn't going to be a little boy. It wasn't bad luck, Devin that I would meet him here after 25 years. It was fate."

171

"He blackmailed you?" Mr Langhar said, his eyes locked with Raphael's. They both seemed to have forgotten everyone else in the room.

"He cornered me the night before the boathouse party. I couldn't help but laugh, within of course- the old man wanted to play games with me? If he knew the truth, he should have known I am not someone to trifle with. It was almost funny, but I was enraged. The plan was already in place," Raphael said with a slight smile on his lips that nothing but the adjective cruel could describe.

"You approached the housekeeper?" Mr Langhar said.

"I could have done it myself, but this was better. No one would tie me to the theft. It was easily arranged. Bhakti stole the pill bottle for me when the American family was out. I had implied I was a drug addict and I needed my fix," Raphael said.

"Then what did you do?"

"Then it was time for that party and a perfect chance. Besides Jeffrey Dale was expecting payment that night, and I was not going to pay him anything."

"You put the drugs in his drink, when?" Mr Langhar asked.

"I was standing at the bar with the Millers, and he walked up to get a drink. I had crushed the pills into a powder beforehand. The lights were dimmed before the announcement to take our seats for the showstopper performance. I moved close to him, to whisper in his ears the assurance that I will have the money ready by tonight and I put the powder in his drink," Raphael said.

"And then you waited for the drugs to do it's job."

"I thought I had put enough. I was sure he would be dead before the party folded. But well not everything could go as planned."

"He left the party immediately after that, and you had no way of knowing the result of your measures," Mr Langhar said.

"It was a very tricky situation. I had to make sure that it was done and dusted. I overheard you and Reece talking about having a nightcap, and I decided to wait it out. I walked on the beach till everything was quiet. Then I swam and went to his villa,"

"You already knew he was a diabetic," Mr Langhar said.

"*Of course, Devin*! It was far easier than the stunt with the pills. The only thing worth regretting is, he died in his sleep. I wanted to make him suffer. He deserved to suffer," Raphael's mouth curled into a cruel grin at the last word.

33

"How did you know it was him?" I asked, stunned.

Raphael Le Gall- a murderer!

"To be honest, it was only suspicion at the beginning. And I had no way of confirming my suspicion. If I had accused without proof, he might have stood the pressure better than he did," Mr Langhar replied.

"But you didn't put any pressure on him," I countered.

Inspector Rashid had made the arrest immediately afterwards. He was standing outside the restaurant with Inspector Hamid. On some cue, they had barged in surprising the guests more than the murderer.

"He was proud of the way he had committed those crimes, the way he had hoodwinked us all. Raphael was eager to show off his brilliance," Mr Langhar said, "I have learned from my experience, the more you assume, the more criminals and people, in general, want to correct you and tell you how they actually did it. It works better than you telling them how you think they did it."

"I got my proof when I saw the photograph. Jeffrey Dale's newspaper had printed a photograph of the victim and the suspect who was a teenager- you remember that photograph?" Mr Langhar said.

"Yeah," I said, thinking back. The young boy who had died- his photograph was a passport-sized picture, but Mason's Hall picture was full-sized. His face showed shock, and it looked as if it had been taken without his consent.

"Raphael had changed so much since then. There was no way anyone could connect him with that old beat-up photo. He told everyone he had never been to America. With his obvious French behaviour, a reasonable person would never doubt him. But he forgot about the scar. It was clearly visible in the picture- that's how Jeffrey Dale recognized him, even after all these years. And that's how I got my proof," Devin Langhar said.

"What about the tiepin we found at Jeffrey's Dale villa? You mean to say he planted that as well to frame Norman Miller?" I asked. That clue cannot be ruled out. It belonged to Norman Miller, and I, for one, don't believe his story about losing it the morning after the murder.

"No, that was the work of Raphael's daughter. Estelle." Mr Langhar said, looking at the corner, where the mother and the daughter were sitting silently.

"You were trying to help your father. Did you see him put the drug in Jeffrey Dale's drink?" Mr Langhar asked.

"You know everything, right? Yes, I was trying to protect someone. I put the tiepin under the bathtub so you could find it. Jason saw me in his villa, and he thought I was stealing the pin," Estelle said, her face a mask of fury and white as a sheet. "But you don't know everything, Mr Langhar. I was trying to protect my mother and not my father."

"Me?" Noemie turned to look at her daughter.

"I saw you walking with that old man on the beach, on the night of the party. And in the morning when I heard that he was dead, I thought that you had killed him. I knew he was a blackmailer. I overheard him blackmailing Mr

175

Miller just that morning. I was scared, and I tried to help you."

"My darling," Noemie Le Gall hugged her daughter closed to her "It wasn't me."

"No it was Evelyn Miller that was walking on the beach with Jeffrey Dale. I don't know if you have noticed, but you Noemie and she look strikingly alike from the back."

I had noticed that at least.

"Why were you arguing with Jason?" I asked Estelle.

"Weren't you listening? He saw me steal his dad's tiepin. He wanted me to go to the Police and tell the truth."

"If only you had come to Police. At least one part of the mystery would have been solved," I said.

"That's why Jason was following you around?" Mr Langhar said.

"He thought I had killed the old man and I wanted to make a scapegoat of his dad," Estelle said.

"Why did you choose the American family? You could have chosen anyone else!" I asked, feeling slightly smug for seeing a point that no one else had seen.

But Estelle looked at me like I was the dumbest person in the room.

"Didn't I just tell you? I heard the old man blackmailing Jason's dad. I knew he had something to hide," Estelle replied, rolling her eyes.

"Shrewd with a strong sense of self-preservation," Mr Langhar muttered more to himself than to the room.

34

The travelling curfew enforced by the Police was finally lifted, and the 6 guests who were not arrested had booked the earliest flight out of this place.

Mr and Mrs Vyas had looked in on us before their departure.

"It was so exciting to see you at the job, Devin! You are a gem of our country," Mr Vyas said, shaking a red-faced Mr Langhar's hand.

"Yes I agree. I will remember this vacation forever. Not because of the charm of Maldives. What an adventure!" Mrs Vyas said, "I do hope to see you again, Devin and you Reece."

Estelle and Noemie Le Gall did not bother with goodbyes. They caught their flight incognito- their oversized sunhat and sunglasses providing ample coverage.

"I need another vacation after this one. This was a busman's holiday," Mr Langhar said.

He and I were standing outside his villa, watching Hassan load his leather bags on the buggy.

"I am never going to an Island again for a holiday. They creep me out," I said. Fat chance I was going to find another employer who would take me for vacations alongside.

"Vacations creep you out?" Mr. Langhar asked.

"No, Islands. It's unnatural."

"I know you are out of a job now. Are you going back to London?"

"Yeah. Fortunately, I had a return ticket. Though I should not use the word fortune or luck in association with me," I moaned.

"Would you like to work as a personal assistant?" Mr Langhar asked, walking towards the buggy.

"For who?" I asked, not trusting my ears.

"Me," Devin Langhar said simply, "You would have to do a little more than you did here. And I demand impeccable standards."

"Mr Langhar, I would be honoured," I said hurriedly, before he could change his mind.

"Great. Report to me at this address in 2 weeks," Mr Langhar said, giving me a card.

"Where are you off to?" I said.

"Weren't you listening? I need another vacation," Devin Langhar said and signalled Hassan to drive the cart.

CPSIA information can be obtained
at www.ICGtesting.com
Printed in the USA
BVHW031407120222
628867BV00013B/164